"I thought you wanted to keep your new life here a secret."

"Some reporter will track me down eventually. This way, I control the situation." Leaning forward, Julia pinned him with a knowing look. "Yesterday, you told me you miss getting the scoop. I'm giving you one, right here, right now. Take it or leave it."

Nick knew if he didn't grab this opportunity, another journalist would. Of course, agreeing meant he'd be stuck in Holiday Harbor longer than he'd planned. But a story like this was worth it. And getting to know the reclusive ambassador's daughter through personal interviews would be downright fascinating.

"Once folks know you're here," he commented, "your online orders should go through the roof."

"I hadn't thought of that. It would be nice to do my books with black ink instead of red."

He scoffed. "Like that's a problem for you."

That got him a steely glare. "Rule number one—assume nothing. Things in my life aren't always what they seem to be."

Books by Mia Ross

Love Inspired

Hometown Family
Circle of Family
A Gift of Family
A Place for Family
*Rocky Coast Romance
*Jingle Bell Romance

*Holiday Harbor

MIA ROSS

loves great stories. She enjoys reading about fascinating people, long-ago times and exotic places. But only for a little while, because her reality is pretty sweet. Married to her college sweetheart, she's the proud mom of two amazing kids, whose schedules keep her hopping. Busy as she is, she can't imagine trading her life for anyone else's—and she has a pretty good imagination. You can visit her online at www.miaross.com.

Jingle Bell Romance

Mia Ross

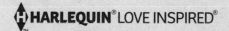
HARLEQUIN® LOVE INSPIRED®

Recycling programs for this product may not exist in your area.

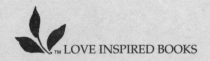

™ LOVE INSPIRED BOOKS

ISBN-13: 978-0-373-81737-5

JINGLE BELL ROMANCE

Copyright © 2013 by Andrea Chermak

All rights reserved. Except for use in any review, the reproduction or utilization of this work in whole or in part in any form by any electronic, mechanical or other means, now known or hereafter invented, including xerography, photocopying and recording, or in any information storage or retrieval system, is forbidden without the written permission of the editorial office, Love Inspired Books, 233 Broadway, New York, NY 10279 U.S.A.

This is a work of fiction. Names, characters, places and incidents are either the product of the author's imagination or are used fictitiously, and any resemblance to actual persons, living or dead, business establishments, events or locales is entirely coincidental.

This edition published by arrangement with Love Inspired Books.

® and TM are trademarks of Love Inspired Books, used under license. Trademarks indicated with ® are registered in the United States Patent and Trademark Office, the Canadian Trade Marks Office and in other countries.

www.Harlequin.com

Printed in U.S.A.

Give, and it will be given to you.
—*Luke* 6:38

For Ruth

Acknowledgments

To the very talented folks who help me make
my books everything they can be: Elaine Spencer,
Melissa Endlich and the dedicated staff
at Love Inspired Books.

More thanks to the gang at Seekerville
(www.seekerville.net). Whether I'm looking for
advice or just some cheerleaders,
you never let me down.

My wonderful—and very patient—
friends and family surround me with support
and encouragement every single day.
Without you, this book would still just be
a quirky idea floating around in my head.

Chapter One

It was the Saturday after Thanksgiving, and Julia Stanton was expecting a busy day at Toyland. Looking forward to some coffee to ward off the chilly morning air, she was about to pull open the door of Holiday Harbor Sweets when a man's black leather glove closed over top of her hand.

"Ladies first," said a deep voice, and she looked up into the darkest brown eyes she'd ever seen. Framed by a tanned face and hair that was just a little too long, those eyes had a piercing quality, as if their owner noticed things other people missed and didn't always like what he saw.

He was wearing classic black, from his briefcase and cashmere dress coat to a pair of stylish boots that were better suited to a business meeting in Manhattan than the slushy sidewalks of northern Maine. Set against the gently falling slow, his outfit gave him a dark, dangerous look. Until he smiled. The gesture lightened his intense features, and unabashed male interest flashed in his eyes.

When he opened the door and motioned her ahead of him, she returned the smile. "Thank you."

"Since I know who you are," he continued while they joined the to-go line, "I'm thinking you know who I am, too."

She laughed. "The notorious Nick McHenry. My friend Bree Landry tells me you're the toughest magazine editor she's ever worked for."

"Aw, she's just being nice. Speaking of Bree, when are she and Cooper due back from their honeymoon in the Caribbean?"

"Her last email said 'in time for Christmas.' That was about a week ago."

"I'm surprised she didn't mention to me that you're living here now. It's not every day you find the daughter of a U.S. Ambassador cooling her heels in a backwater place like this."

His unmasked disdain for the quaint village she'd called home for six months irked her to say the least. "Why would you say that? I thought you grew up here."

"I did. First chance I got, I was outta here."

"Too bad you didn't stay out." A young woman interrupted their conversation with an unforgiving scowl. Normally sweet and cheerful, Lucy

Wilson looked as if she'd just run across her worst enemy.

"Hey there, Lucky," Nick replied. "How've you been?"

"I know you and your idiot buddies all thought that was funny in high school," she snarled, "but it wasn't. It's even less funny now."

"Right. Sorry." His brush-off tone made it clear he wasn't sorry at all, and Julia couldn't understand why he seemed to be going out of his way to make Lucy angry.

"What are you doing here anyway?" Lucy demanded.

"Mom invited me up for Thanksgiving," he replied smoothly, not showing the tiniest bit of concern about the bitter reception he'd gotten. "You wouldn't want me to disappoint her, would you?"

"You haven't been back in what? Seven years?" she challenged him. "Why now?"

For the first time, the seemingly unflappable man showed irritation with her less-than-welcoming attitude. "Planning to showcase my personal business on page one of the local paper again?"

Julia couldn't imagine why on earth they were going at it in public this way. She was starting to feel uncomfortable standing in the middle of this showdown, but there was no polite way to walk away.

"That was ages ago, and you totally deserved it."

Still locked in a glaring contest with her, he said, "Not that anyone around here will care, but I wanted to meet my niece and nephew."

"Whatever. Take my word on this one," she cautioned Julia. "He's been nothing but trouble his whole life."

Julia glanced at him, and he nodded solemnly in agreement. His glum expression was clearly an act, though. The bemused twinkle in his eyes gave him away. Without another word, Lucy shoved past him and charged out the door without ordering anything. The overhead bells jangled sharply as she left, and Julia faced Nick with a frown of her own. "You were needling her on purpose."

There was that wicked grin again. "Yeah."

"Why on earth would you do that? Especially this time of year."

"You mean because it's Christmas?" When she nodded, he shrugged. "To me, vacation's over, and I've got a ton of work to do. I need a bagel, some decent coffee and a wireless connection so I can plow through the pile of emails I haven't been able to read since I got here Wednesday. I don't have time to make nice with someone who's determined to hate me no matter what I say or do."

Julia was confused. "Why haven't you been able to check your email? I thought you were staying with your sister, Lainie, and her family."

"I am." He gave her a suspicious look that appeared so natural for him, she assumed it was his normal way of interacting with people he'd just met. "How did you know that?"

"When I moved here in the spring, I didn't know anyone, and she took me under her wing. She and I have gotten to be good friends. She told me you were coming and would be staying with them. I know they have wireless at their house."

"Sure, but no privacy. I can't concentrate with everyone yakking all the time."

Why had he even bothered to come back? she wondered. The holidays were for family, but aside from the comment about meeting his niece and nephew, he didn't seem to appreciate that at all.

Not her concern, she reminded herself sternly. If he wanted to neglect his relatives, that was his own business.

They moved up a spot in line, and Julia told him, "There's no internet in here."

"I know, but someone around here must've smartened up by now. Know any place in this map dot town that's made it into the twenty-first century?"

Julia had the kind of connection he needed at her shop, but she was hesitant to tell him so. If she did, it would be common courtesy to allow him to use it, and she wasn't at all certain she wanted him camped out in her store on such a busy shopping day. With his brooding vibe and incessant grumbling, he'd probably scare away half her customers.

You get what you give, Julia.

In her memory, she heard her mother's gentle voice repeating one of her personal philosophies. Gisele Stanton had lived her entire life that way, abandoning a promising orchestral career to accompany her ambassador husband to every corner of the globe. While Julia had no intention of putting aside her own wishes for anyone ever again, she always did her best to follow her mother's generous example.

"I have wireless at Toyland," she finally said before she could think better of it. "You're welcome to use it—with one condition."

"Twenty bucks a minute?"

While she knew he was joking, the cynical remark spoke volumes about how this jaded journalist viewed the world. "You have to buy a toy to place under my Gifting Tree. They'll go to local children to make their Christmas a little brighter."

He blinked. Charity appeared to be a foreign concept to him. "You're kidding."

"Not at all." She gave him her sweetest smile, the one that over the years had charmed countless dignitaries and a crown prince or two. "That's the deal—take it or leave it."

"Next!"

Eyeing Julia incredulously, Nick turned to the young woman behind the counter. Dressed in a red-and-green-striped shirt and fuzzy stocking cap, she tilted her head expectantly. "What can I get you?"

He rattled off a complex order, and she laughed. "You're kidding, right? I don't know what half that stuff is."

"Fine." His jaw tightened, as if he was struggling to keep control of what seemed to be a remarkably short temper. "What've you got?"

"Regular or decaf, large or small. I've got some choco-peppermint holiday creamer if you want that."

His grimace made it clear he wanted nothing to do with creamer, holiday or otherwise. "I'll take a large regular, black, with a poppy seed bagel." At her give-me-a-break look, he sighed. "Plain bagel."

"Coming right up."

He didn't respond, but as the overhead speakers crackled with "Deck the Halls," he groaned softly. "This Podunk town wouldn't know a latte or decent music if someone force-fed it to them."

Because she was far from perfect, Julia made it a habit to be tolerant of other people's shortcomings. But his constant griping was getting on her nerves. "Not a morning person, Mr. McHenry?"

"Not a Christmas person," he corrected her as

he reached into his inner coat pocket for his designer wallet. "Lainie calls me Scrooge, and she's not far off. I'm not into the decorations and sappy carols and all that. Never have been, never will be."

She waited a moment, then attempted to lighten the mood with, "Aren't you going to say 'bah, humbug'?"

He replied only with a wry grin, and she wondered if he enjoyed his Scrooge-y demeanor. He certainly had no qualms about showing his more abrasive side. Although she was still new in town, something told her Lucy wasn't the only local resident who wouldn't be pleased to see him. In a few short minutes, Julia had discovered he had a bristly personality and a sharp tongue. Honing that kind of sarcasm must have taken years, and she suspected he'd never been one who played well with others.

"This is such a wonderful time of year," she said gently while he paid for his order. "I can't imagine why you hate it so much."

"Trust me. You'd rather not know."

He didn't elaborate, and Julia moved up to take his place at the front of the line. "Just the usual, Ellen. Thanks."

Nick stood to the side but leaned in to add, "Miss Stanton's order is on me."

"Okay."

Ellen scurried off to fill a take-out bag, and Julia looked at Nick. "That's really not necessary."

"You're helping me out, so I figure it's the least I can do."

Baffled by his sudden shift in attitude from grim to generous, she smiled and offered her hand. "Then it's Julia."

"And I'm Nick." Mischief brightened his features as they shook. "Does this mean you're ignoring Lucy's warning about me?"

"For now." It was hard to resist the glimmer in his eyes, but she did her best. This guy probably had women fawning all over him on a daily basis. She didn't want to give him any reason to think she'd be doing the same. "I like her very much, but I make up my own mind about people."

Ellen returned with her breakfast, and Julia thanked her, taking the bag and cup while Nick paid. He added a nice tip, then angled to the side to allow Julia to leave the store in front of him.

Out on the sidewalk, a cold gust of wind hit them, and he shuddered. "Man, I hate winter."

"Really? I love it." To prove her point, she took in a deep breath of crisp, cool Maine air. "It smells clean and fresh, like anything's possible."

"It smells cold," he muttered, glaring at the lazily falling snow as if he could will it to stop. "I'm headed back to Richmond today."

"What a fabulous city, with all that history,"

she commented, hoping to draw him into a more pleasant conversation. "How long have you been living there?"

He shrugged. "A year, I guess."

"Virginia is a long way from here. What made you choose it?"

"No special reason. I just kept moving south 'til I found a spot where I can stand all the seasons."

He didn't sound all that thrilled with where he'd landed, and she wondered if he was still searching for a permanent place to live. Then again, maybe he didn't even want to settle down. Having moved from one diplomatic post to another with her parents, the gypsy lifestyle no longer appealed to her. Still, she could understand how the excitement of it might be attractive to someone else.

Since Nick was clearly happy to be on his way out of town, there was no point in probing any further. Unfortunately, that meant she'd drained her usual well of small talk, and she was relieved when they reached her shop.

They paused outside the antique door, and Nick held their food while she dug out her keys. When she looked up, she noticed his eyes were fixed on the simple white church across the square. "Pretty, isn't it?" she asked.

"My father's church," he replied in a clipped tone. "But if you asked him, I doubt he'd claim me. I'm the black sheep of the clan."

Delivered in a near monotone, she couldn't decide if the confession pained him or angered him. The flash of anger in his eyes answered that question better than any words. "I attend services there, and I enjoy his sermons very much," Julia said.

"I can't say the same." Nick's face twisted into something between a smirk and a scowl. "I guess they're easier to take when they're not aimed at you."

Attempting to redirect the conversation, she said, "It's a lovely church, with all that leaded glass and hand-carved woodwork. I've always been curious about who built it."

His nasty expression faded, and he met her eyes calmly. "You've been here long enough to know the Landrys built it in 1817, a year after they got here."

"On Christmas Day," she added. "Which is how the town got its name."

"You're just trying to distract me with this little history lesson."

For some reason, he was trying to start a fight with her. Rather than join in, she laughed. "Is it working?"

That got her a slow easy smile, completely at odds with the intensity she'd assumed was part of his personality. A pleasant surprise, it brightened his gloomy expression. "Let's just say I could think of worse ways to kill a few hours before my flight than spending it with such a beautiful woman."

His rapidly shifting moods set off alarm bells in her head, making her wonder what else he was hiding beneath that cool, detached exterior. Shaking off the thought, she cautioned herself that he was too arrogant to interest her.

She'd spent most of her twenty-eight years traveling the world, and she'd run across more than her share of alpha males along the way. The last one—a dashing Italian banker—all but destroyed her life before vanishing into thin air. Thanks to him, she'd given up on men a long time ago. Especially men like Nick, who clearly had no intention of sticking around.

Although he'd grown up here, Nick felt more claustrophobic than ever.

Perched on the rocky Atlantic coast, the village had been built around a town square with a white gazebo currently draped with fresh pine boughs. Up and down Main Street, shops and businesses were decorated with multi-colored garlands and twinkling lights. The snow drifting from the sky added to the effect, bringing to mind one of those Currier and Ives cards people loved to send him this time of year.

Holiday shopping wouldn't be exactly like it

was in other places, with crazed customers and twenty-four-hour sales, but for the handful of retail stores it would make or break their winter.

A cherry picker stopped at the far end of the short business district, and a guy wearing a hard hat climbed into the bucket with an armful of lighted garlands. They'd be looped in several spots across the width of Main Street, the way they'd been every year since Nick could remember.

That was the biggest problem with this town. Nothing ever changed.

Almost nothing, he amended as Julia unlocked the door and he followed her inside. He'd seen a lot since leaving for college at NYU, and not much surprised him anymore. Finding Julia Stanton here definitely fell into that category. Mostly because he couldn't begin to comprehend why she'd chosen to settle down here of all places. Wealthy and connected beyond belief, she could have her pick of any glamorous city on the planet.

Why Holiday Harbor?

The reporter in him loved contradiction because they always led him in unexpected directions. These days, he spent more time editing articles, courting advertisers and designing copy layouts than writing, but the newshound in him smelled a story.

Standing in the entryway, he paused to take

in the two giant Christmas trees framed in the display windows on either side of the glass-front door. A vintage train circled beneath one, snaking through festively wrapped gifts that reflected the bright lights and decorations. Under the other tree was a miniature version of Holiday Harbor, complete with ersatz snow, a skating pond and a white chapel lit from inside. Light glowed in the opaque windows, giving them the appearance of candlelight.

His father's church, he noted grimly. As if seeing the real thing hadn't been jarring enough. When he leaned closer, he saw that the gold lettering on the tiny sign read, "Safe Harbor Church. All are welcome."

All but him. In an instant, his mind flashed back to childhood days spent in that church. Sitting in the front pew where Dad could keep a stern eye on him, make sure he didn't daydream through endless sermons about saints and sinners, and how God knew what was in your heart. Week after week, year after year, he'd endured it because he hadn't had a choice. His father never struck him, never raised his voice in anger, but he beat Nick down with God's word, an inch at a time.

His own son, Nick recalled with a flare of anger, but not his favorite son. Not even close.

Feeling ambushed by the replica, he cooled his

spiking temper with a deep breath. It was a lifetime ago, he reminded himself. He was twenty-eight now, and those oppressive memories were in the past. He'd worked hard to put them behind him, and they couldn't hurt him anymore unless he allowed them to.

"Nick?" Hearing Julia's voice, he dragged his eyes from the seemingly idyllic scene. "Are you okay?"

"Sure. Just admiring your handiwork. Very pretty."

She gave him the kind of long, mistrustful look he'd gotten from more women than he cared to recall. Normally, he shrugged them off and moved on, but for some reason, coming from her it bothered him. He couldn't imagine why he cared what she thought of him, but he did, just the same.

"Really?" she asked. "I thought you hated all this."

"I kind of said that, didn't I?"

"Yes, you did, right after you called yourself a Scrooge."

He didn't often regret anything, but as she frowned at him now, he wished he could take back the offhand remark. "Well, it's not usually my thing, but the way you do it isn't so bad."

She gave him a quick once-over that made him want to squirm. "You're trying to butter me up, aren't you?"

Busted, he thought, hoping to turn things around with a smile. "Maybe a little."

Shaking her head, she returned the smile, and he congratulated himself on smoothing over a potentially awkward situation. She'd been nice to him, and he found himself wanting to follow her example. Far from his usual keep-your-distance policy, it felt strange, but he could put up with it for the short time he'd be here.

As he glanced around, he noticed that the vaulted ceilings in the turn-of-the-century building allowed enough height to have a narrow walkway above. Dozens of tiny colored lights were draped along the railing, and between the posts she'd posed a stuffed version of every animal he'd ever seen. And even some he hadn't.

"What's that?" he asked, pointing at a scruffy-looking critter dangling from the top rail.

"A tree sloth. The one underneath is a ground sloth, crawling over to say hello to his friends the gorilla and the toucan. They're discussing what to get Tarzan for Christmas."

Without her ivory wool coat and hat, she was a dead ringer for Grace Kelly, his all-time favorite actress. More than beautiful, she always played classy characters with a surprising backbone underneath all that polish. Nick seldom considered it necessary to look beyond a woman's appearance, but he couldn't help wondering if Julia shared Grace's steely quality.

With her blond hair pulled back in a gold barrette, she was dressed in gray trousers and a simple ivory sweater that made her eyes look even bluer than they had earlier. Nick didn't know if it was the lady herself or all the lights, but in here, those eyes twinkled with a childlike enthusiasm.

It contradicted every impression he'd formed of her from press releases over the years. She was more than the cool, privileged ambassador's daughter the media portrayed her as, which only made her more fascinating to him. "You really thought this over, didn't you?"

"Kids have such great imaginations," she replied, gliding past him to adjust the flame in the cheery gas fireplace. "I want them to have fun here, so I make up stories about the toys. They seem to like it."

He didn't normally give children much thought, but he heard himself ask, "Who wouldn't? It's like a winter wonderland in here."

"That's the idea."

She rewarded him with a warm, approving look that made him want another one. Searching his mind, he came up with a surefire strategy. "Seeing as I'm a Scrooge who's never even set foot in a toy store, what would you recommend for me to put under the gifting tree?"

"The children fill out a tag for something that would make their Christmas morning special." She pointed to yet another tree set up near the fireplace. Decorated in a more casual style, it sported at least a dozen sparkly snowflakes with writing on them. "The only rule is, nothing practical. No socks or school supplies. It has to be something they really, truly want just because it would make them happy. With the economy the way it is, lots of parents have a tough time buying anything beyond the necessities."

"So you're filling in the gap."

"I'm trying to."

What a nice thing to do. Most of the women he met were either obsessed with their own careers or determined to snag a man who could support them with his. Finding one who seemed to fall in neither of those columns intrigued him, to say the least. Nick strolled over to the tree, figuring it shouldn't be too hard to hold up his end of the bargain. He'd pick one, buy the gift and then get to work. But as he surveyed the tags, his plans quickly got derailed.

"A stuffed puppy," one read, "because Mommy says we can't buy food for a real one."

"A collar with a name tag for my kitten," another said, "because she's my best friend, and I don't want her to get lost."

One in particular caught his eye because he

recognized his niece Hannah's writing from the artwork plastering the front of his sister's fridge. Taking it from the branch, he read the misspelled request. "Ples brng uncl nik hom to liv. Momy and grama mis him."

Not Grampa, though. Even four-year-old Hannah had picked up on the rift in the family, Nick thought as he showed the tag to Julia. "Did you see this one?"

"Yes. Lainie and Todd brought the kids in Wednesday morning to wish me a Happy Thanksgiving."

"Hannah just met me," he protested. "Why would she wish for me to come home?"

Julia tilted her head at him with a sympathetic expression. "She's a sweet little girl, and she wants to make her family happy."

"Well, I'm not staying." Crushing the cut-out snowflake in his fist, he jammed it into the pocket of his coat. Although he couldn't fulfill his niece's request, he didn't want her to be disappointed on Christmas Day. "You should have her make another tag so she gets something else."

"You could compromise by staying a few more days," Julia suggested while she wired holly berries into one of the display wreaths. "Let her get to know you and vice versa. You might even enjoy yourself."

She didn't seem to be listening to him, so Nick

was fairly certain he'd never be able to make this kind woman see his point of view. Out of long-standing habit, he went with bravado. "That's not gonna happen. I have a business to get back to."

She pressed her perfectly curved lips into a dis-approving line but didn't say anything more on the subject. Ending the argument had been Nick's intent, but he had to admit her quick surrender was a letdown. Not that it mattered, of course. He'd just been hoping she'd give him more of a challenge.

"You can set yourself up in my office." She pointed to a burgundy velvet curtain held aside by gold tassels. "It's back through there."

"Thanks, but I need to buy a toy first."

"Don't worry about it." Flicking her hand, she set a gold charm bracelet jingling like a set of sleigh bells. "I know you're anxious to get out of town, so I won't hold you up."

He wasn't crazy about choosing a gift for some rug rat he didn't even know, so Nick was thrilled to be let off the hook so easily. He hurried toward the back of the store before she could change her mind. As he pulled his laptop from its case, Nick was disturbed to find he was still rattled by Han-nah's Christmas wish. She was so young, he was sure his sister hadn't filled her in on the darker side of the McHenry family history. It was hard for grown-ups to handle, and he wouldn't wish it on a child.

He was objective and logical by nature. Ideal for a reporter, those qualities also served him well in his personal relationships. He kept people—including his family—at arm's length because he'd learned that was the best way to get through life unscathed. Since they'd just met, Julia didn't know that, and even if he managed to find a way to explain, she wouldn't understand. Open and gracious, she was his polar opposite, like sunshine bringing light to a cloudy day.

Completely out of character for him, the poetic image didn't do much for his mood, and he grumbled as he settled in at Julia's desk and powered up his computer. Hopefully, focusing on work would get his mind off the clash of emotions Hannah's innocent request had unleashed inside him.

His quick trip to the toy store had turned into more than he'd planned on, and he didn't like it. Not one bit.

Chapter Two

Julia was hanging stockings on the mantel when she felt a tug on the hem of her sweater. She didn't recognize the little boy, but he had a shy look about him, so she hunkered down to his level. "May I help you, sir?"

"My friend told me you're doing ging-a-bread houses," he answered so quietly she had to strain to hear him.

"Yes, we are." Noticing his mother hovering nearby, she smiled at the young woman, then at her son. "Every Saturday from two to five, starting next week. Did you want to make one? I can add you to our list."

His hazel eyes big as saucers, he nodded solemnly. "My name is Colby."

As he stared at her, Julia got the feeling he wanted to say something else, but she didn't want to rush him. A timid soul herself, she resented it when people hurried her through a conversation or—worse yet—presumed they knew what she was thinking. So she took her time writing his name on the schedule.

A few seconds later, he rewarded her patience. "Do you have any more of those trucks?"

He pointed to an antique model from Berlin. Part of Julia's private collection, it was one-of-a-kind and not for sale. Judging by his mother's panicky look, she'd already guessed that.

Julia eased her mind with a wink, then spoke to her son. "Actually, that's the last one. I found it at a store in Germany, and I've been saving it for someone special. Do you think maybe that's you?"

"Yes," he replied, quickly this time. "It's just like the one my granddad used to drive when he helped build the road out to Schooner Point. He showed me pictures…"

Delighted that he'd opened up to her, Julia listened while Colby relayed some of what his grandfather had told him about working on the road crew. When he was finished, she took a blank snowflake from the basket on the counter. "To get the truck, you need to fill this out for me and hang it on the Gifting Tree. In return, bring in a small gift for someone else to make their Christmas better. Okay?"

He checked with his mom, who looked a little

shocked but nodded. While he was occupied filling out his tag, she moved closer to Julia. "How did you do that?" she asked in a hushed tone. "He never talks to anyone outside the family."

Laughing, Julia patted her arm. "Boys and trucks. Or lizards or snakes, or something like that."

"How many children do you have?"

The innocent question plucked a painful nerve, but Julia covered it with a smile. "None. I just like kids."

Glancing around, the young mother leaned in closer. "I have to say, I've heard some not very nice things about you since you moved here in the spring. But that truck must've been expensive, and you're very generous to give it to a little boy you don't even know. I'm glad to find out those folks were wrong."

Time and again Julia had endured the snap judgments people made about her simply because they assumed she must be snobby and spoiled because she was rich and famous. She'd come to this picturesque village, far removed from the public eye, intending to erase all that and start again. Unfortunately, it was easier said than done.

"Hopefully, once they get to know me, they'll feel the same way," she commented as Colby rejoined his mother.

"I know they will. Thanks again."

As the two of them made their way out, she heard him say, "Mommy, I like that pretty toy lady."

The sweet comment made her smile, and Julia went to help another customer trying to choose between lawyer Barbie and ballerina Barbie. They were debating which would appeal most to her seven-year-old granddaughter when a frustrated bellow shook the Austrian crystal ornaments dangling from one of the trees.

"What do you mean, cancelled?"

The elderly woman gave Julia a hawkish look. "You have a man back there?"

"No." Realizing that sounded dishonest, she immediately corrected herself. "Well, yes, but he's just using my office to get some work done. Excuse me a minute."

"No rush." Holding a box in each hand, she looked from one to the other. "I need to think about this."

"Take your time." Hurrying to the back, Julia wished she'd installed a door to contain the noise. Since she and a couple of part-time clerks were the only ones who worked in the store, it hadn't seemed necessary. Until now.

Hoping to avoid a further scene, she kept her voice low as she entered. "Is there a problem back here?"

Clearly aggravated, a scowling Nick waved her

off. Pinching the bridge of his nose between his fingers, he growled, "I know there's a storm coming up the coast. That's why I'm trying to get back to Richmond. Today." He listened for a few moments, then heaved a long-suffering sigh. "Fine, tomorrow at noon. I don't care how much more it is—just get me on that flight."

Clicking his phone off, he tossed it on Julia's small writing desk in a gesture she presumed was commonplace for him. Irked by his rudeness, she rested a protective hand on one of her prized possessions. "This was handmade for me by an artisan in Tuscany. I'd appreciate you not beating on it because you're mad."

"Sorry." Another deep sigh, and he glowered up at the ceiling, as if that would get his plane back on schedule. He blinked, then did a slow circuit of the high shelves that made it clear he'd just noticed them. "Whoa. That's a lot of— What are they?"

"Dollhouse miniatures," she replied, handing his phone back to him. "I've been collecting them since I was a little girl."

There was at least one complete set of every room in a doll's mansion, down to the real silverware, china and delicate crystal set for twelve on a Chippendale dining table. Four-poster beds, sofas and chairs, electric lamps of all sizes, even three vintage bathrooms—all arranged in vignettes she lovingly dusted once a week.

Glancing around, he came back to her with a puzzled expression. "Where's the dollhouse?"

"We traveled so much when I was growing up, it didn't make sense to constantly pack and unpack something that big. I collected small things, so I could always take them with me. Now that I'm settled, I'd love to get a dollhouse but haven't had the chance yet."

"No pets with all that moving around, huh?"

"Oh, no, we had lots of pets. My mother loves birds, and we always had a cat or two." Thinking back through her father's many assignments, she laughed. "In Australia, we took care of an orphaned koala until it was old enough to go into the reserve."

"Very cool," he breathed, and a quick glance told her he meant it. Unfortunately, his next comment ruined the moment. "Y'know, you'd make a great article. Glamorous world traveler bringing Christmas to kids in a small town, something like that. With your connections to famous entertainers, politicians and royalty, your story would be picked up by every media service in the world."

"My life was on display for years, but I'm done with that," she informed him crisply as she turned to go. "While you're in my office, please keep your voice down."

Unfazed by her scolding, he pointed at her with a shameless wink. "Gotcha."

Lucy was right, Julia fumed as she pulled herself back together and returned to her confused customer. Nick McHenry was nothing but trouble.

"G'bye, Uncle Nick." Sunday morning, Hannah wrapped her arms around his legs, which was as high as she could reach. "See you at Christmas."

Bag in one hand, he patted her head with the other. "I might not be able to do that, munchkin. I appreciate the invitation, though."

As Hannah went back into the living room to watch some kids' TV show, he glanced over at his little sister, including her in the apology. Lainie looked unhappy but nodded because that was the answer she'd expected. She didn't like it, but she understood.

"Thanks for coming," she said, giving him his third hug of the day. "It meant a lot to Mom and me."

But not to Dad, Nick added silently. While he'd anticipated the pastor's cool reception and barely there conversation, it had stung more than he wanted to admit. So many years had passed since they'd been together as a family, he'd let himself believe that maybe this visit would be different.

Wrong again.

His phone started buzzing in his coat pocket. Grateful for the distraction, he took it out and checked the caller ID. When he saw it was the Rockland Airport, he groaned before hitting Answer. "Please don't tell me that Richmond flight's delayed again."

Feeling like the universe itself was somehow lined up against him, he leaned his forehead against a cool pane of glass in the kitchen door. Yesterday's flurries had built into something more substantial, and he heard the scraping-ice sound of a highway plow passing by the house. "I know the weather's still bad. When's the first plane back?"

Grinding his teeth, he waited while the airline clerk tapped keys on her computer. Her eventual answer didn't thrill him. Apparently they were grounding all flights south, and the first flight out was— "Noon tomorrow? Are you serious?"

After being assured that yes, the clerk was serious, he sighed his agreement and scribbled his new confirmation code on the back of the tag he'd crammed into his pocket at the toy store and promptly forgotten. Punching the off button on his phone, he put it back in his pocket and waved the snowflake at Lainie. "Did you know about this?"

In the middle of washing the breakfast dishes, she let her hands drip into the sink and looked over at him. "Sure. Julia told Hannah she could ask for anything she wanted, and she asked for you."

"That's crazy," he grumbled, dropping into one of six mismatched chairs. "She doesn't even know me."

Taking a towel from its ring near the sink, Lainie dried her hands before joining him at the table. Resting a hand on his arm, she gave him an adoring smile. "She knows *about* you. I've got plenty of pictures, and I've told her lots of stories about her supersmart and talented uncle. I mean, how many people have what it takes to run their very own online magazine?"

Her glowing description of him made him antsy, and he leaned back in his chair to put a little space between them. "Thanks, but I kinda like my black-sheep status. Makes things easier."

"Things like ducking every family gathering for the past seven years? After you came back for my wedding, it was like you dropped off the face of the earth." Frowning, she shook her head. "That's no way to live, Nick. Mom and I miss you like crazy."

"Not Dad, though," he argued. "He likes this arrangement just as much as I do."

"It's not an arrangement. It's avoidance, and I don't understand why the rest of us have to suffer because you and Dad are too stubborn to make amends."

"Amends?" Instantly on the defensive, Nick jumped up to start pacing. "What makes you think that's even possible after all this time?"

"Ian's death was an accident. Everyone knows that except you."

Normally, he avoided this subject entirely, but for some reason today was different. "It wasn't an accident, and Dad and I both know it. I'm responsible for what happened. If I hadn't been messing around in that boat, our big brother would've had a great life instead of drowning when he was fifteen."

Anguish filled her hazel eyes, then tears began streaming down her cheeks. Nick felt awful for having unleashed all that, and he crouched down to put a hand on her shoulder. "I'm sorry, Lainie. I didn't mean to open all that up again."

"It's not your fault." She sniffled, gazing at him with the loving little-sister look he'd missed all these years. "It was never your fault. Every night, I pray that someday you'll believe that."

She meant well, and the thought of her praying for him should have made him feel better. Instead, it shoved his temper into high gear, and he fought to keep his voice calm. "Save your prayers for someone who really needs them. I'm fine."

"No, you're not," she insisted with the same

trademark McHenry stubbornness she'd accused him of. "I don't care how indestructible you think you are. No one's strong enough to handle everything on their own."

"It's a nice thought." Standing, he kissed her forehead before stepping back. "But you're wasting your time praying for me."

Gasping, she stared at him as if he'd slapped her. "How could you possibly think that?"

"God only answers if He cares. He stopped caring about me a long time ago."

Because he'd had more than enough theology for one day, Nick pulled up his coat collar and headed outside. It would be cold out there, but at least it would be quiet.

After an enjoyable but exhausting Saturday at Toyland, Julia welcomed the quiet of Sunday morning. Walking to the small church across the square, she met up with several others doing the same thing. They all greeted her with a smile, and they chatted along the way. A weekly tradition for her, it was a very pleasant start to the day.

Inside the old-fashioned chapel, Julia slid into her usual spot beside the Martins. After greeting everyone, she glimpsed the pastor's wife, Ann McHenry, sitting with the choir and sent her a subtle wave. The woman beamed and nodded back, and Julia realized she was looking into the same eyes Nick had. The difference was that Ann's had a permanent sparkle in them, as if she looked into the world and saw something amusing every day.

Her son's held barely restrained contempt, with the occasional glint of interest when something snared his attention. During her life in the diplomatic arena, Julia had met hundreds of people, and she'd developed a knack for reading them. None of that helped her with Nick, she thought with a frown as she opened her hymnal. From what she'd seen, the man was a mystery wrapped in an enigma.

"Did Nick get to the airport all right?" she asked Lainie.

"His flight got delayed 'til tomorrow. He stayed up late working last night, so he was still asleep when we left to come here. He probably wouldn't have come anyway," she added with a grimace. "Stubborn's not the word for him sometimes."

Julia had no trouble believing that, but she suspected his challenging demeanor was his way of keeping people at a distance. Sadly, it was a strategy she understood all too well. Trusting by nature, she'd learned the hard way that when you let someone too close, they discovered all kinds of things about you. That kind of intimate knowledge gave them a chance to hurt you so deeply, it took all your strength just to put one foot in front of the other.

The organ's mellow chords pulled her from her dismal thoughts, and she gladly let them go. After their first hymn, Pastor Daniel McHenry moved out from behind his lectern and held his arms open wide. "Welcome, one and all, to the Safe Harbor Church. If you're joining us for the first time this morning, feel free to introduce yourself."

It was a no-pressure way to bring them into the fold, and the few brave enough to stand were greeted warmly by the pastor. She'd never known Pastor McHenry to have a harsh word for anyone. His wife and daughter were the same way. So what had happened with Nick? It must have been something horrible to drive a wedge so firmly between him and his father.

"Today's sermon comes from Luke and is inspired by my very generous wife." Pausing, he smiled back at Ann before facing the gathering again. "Give, and it will be given to you."

The line reminded Julia of her mother's gentle advice, and she listened closely as he continued with a lesson about giving of yourself to make God's world a better place. "Generosity isn't only for the wealthy with money to spare," he reminded them. "Share what you have—your time, your skills, your patience—to make someone else's life better. That," he assured them, "is Jesus's enduring message, and the true spirit of Christmas."

Julia normally had no trouble following the pastor's heartfelt sermons, but her mind kept drifting to the new impressions she'd gotten of his family since meeting Nick. Every family had their troubles, but the McHenrys' seemed to run much deeper than most. From the sketchy details Lainie had shared about her brother, Julia gathered that she and her mom had given up on fixing the problem between the father and son and were settling for civility on the few occasions they were forced to be together.

Throughout his distinguished career, Julia's father had brought countless adversaries together to devise an acceptable truce between them. Some situations required more effort than others, but his remarkable success with sworn enemies spoke for itself. Over the years, she'd picked up some of those skills from observing him and often used them with people who seemed intent on making her life difficult. Could she use those skills here?

Lainie nudged her, and Julia stood for the next hymn. When her friend gave her a puzzled look, Julia simply smiled back. Unlike so many others, the Martins and McHenrys hadn't labeled her a spoiled rich girl based on her nice clothes and exotic jewelry. Instead, they'd taken the time to get to know her and had made her feel like part of their family. Grateful beyond words, she wanted to do something that would make this Christmas extra special for them.

In that moment, it came to her. Of all the gifts she could give them, Julia knew which one would mean the most.

She'd broker peace between Nick and his father.

Nick himself had set the wheels in motion by coming home for Thanksgiving. To Julia, that proved the situation wasn't entirely hopeless, but she recognized she couldn't manage such a monumental task on her own.

Looking up, she closed her eyes and silently prayed for help in mending the McHenrys' broken family. After a few moments, a sense of calm settled over her, assuring her she'd been heard and an answer was on the way.

Chapter Three

When Nick stepped outside to check on the snow-fall, he heard the chorus of "Rudolph" coming from across the yard and found his brother-in-law singing along with the radio while he shoveled the driveway. Todd Martin was new in town, which in Holiday Harbor meant he'd been around less than ten years, arriving after Nick had left for New York. While Todd must have had heard plenty of negative things about him, apparently he didn't hold any of them against Nick.

"You know that's a losing cause around here, right?" Nick teased.

Todd laughed. "Yeah, but someone's gotta do it. Lainie's with the kids, so I'm elected."

"In that case, do you have another shovel?"

Glancing at Nick's stylish leather boots, he grinned. "You're not exactly dressed for man-ual labor."

"I'll be fine." Noticing a smaller shovel leaning against the shed, he retrieved it and started in on the other side of the driveway.

"Thanks for the help." As they got to work, Todd continued. "I heard you're stuck here 'til tomorrow."

"Yeah. If I'd known how long I'd be here, I'd have stayed at a hotel so I wouldn't be in your way."

"What makes you think you're in the way?"

When Nick didn't answer, Todd abruptly stopped working and waited for Nick to look at him. "Lainie told me what happened to Ian and how things went for your family afterward. That has nothing to do with me, and I'm not one to judge anyway."

It was one of the nicest things anyone had said to him all week, and Nick smiled. "I appreciate that."

"From what I see, you're a decent guy, and having you around makes my wife happy. We've got a perfectly good guest room here, and you're welcome to it as long as you want to stay."

"Thanks, Todd."

"Don't mention it." Grinning, he picked up his shovel again. "I have to admit, it's nice having another pair of hands out here. Hannah tries, but after a few minutes, she starts making snow angels and throwing snowballs. Then we end up in a snowball fight, and I'm out here 'til dark."

So he dropped what he was doing when his daughter wanted to play, then worked longer to get the job done. That was how a father should be, and Nick admired Todd's devotion to his family. Imagining them playing in the snow brought to mind the Christmas cards that always stacked up on his hall table until he finally tossed them out on New Year's Day.

Even though the Martins' humble lifestyle was starkly different from his own, Nick felt himself smiling back. "Sounds like fun."

"Yeah, it is. I can't wait until Noah's older, and all four of us can play."

"Girls against the guys?"

"Got that right."

"Just watch out for Lainie," Nick warned as a silver Mercedes pulled into the cleared half of the driveway. "She plays dirty."

The car glided to a stop, and when the driver's door opened, Nick was stunned to see Holiday Harbor's favorite toy store owner stepping out. Assessing their progress, she smiled over at them. "Good work."

"Thanks," Todd said, strolling over to greet her. "I figure we'll be done right about the time the next storm comes through."

She laughed, and the bright sound struck Nick

as a perfect accompaniment to the Christmas music on the radio. "Isn't that always the way?"

"Seems to be." Seeming to remember he had company, Todd added, "Where are my manners? Julia Stanton, this is Lainie's brother, Nick McHenry."

"We met in town yesterday," she said politely.

Usually adept at reading between the lines, Nick couldn't get a handle on how she felt about their unusual encounter. While she gave the appearance of being open and friendly, she actually kept her emotions well masked. Must be all that diplomatic training, he decided. She could probably turn that stunning movie-star charisma of hers on and off at will. "Nice to see you again."

"And you, as well." Opening the passenger door of her car, she pulled out a bag imprinted with Toyland in the same gold script lettering he'd noticed at the shop. "The girls have things under control at the shop, so I'm on a delivery run."

Nick let out a low whistle. "That's what I call service."

"When you have young children, it's hard to keep their gifts a surprise," she explained in an ultrapatient tone she probably used with troublesome customers in her store. Not rude, exactly, but it lacked the warmth she'd shown his brother-in-law.

"That's the truth." Taking the bag, Todd added,

"I'll hide them in my workshop. Hannah's not al-lowed in there, so they'll be safe."

Nick didn't understand why they were going to so much trouble to keep the presents a secret. Maybe it was something you didn't understand until you joined the parent club. Then again, Julia didn't have children, but she seemed to buy into it completely. So maybe, he admitted with a mental sigh, it was just him.

"I'm ready for a break," Todd continued. "I'll stash these and meet you inside."

Julia checked her slender gold wristwatch. "I really should get back."

"We've got hot cocoa," he pressed, adding a pleading look. "If Lainie and Hannah find out I let you leave without saying hello, I'll never hear the end of it."

"All right, then," she relented with a smile. "I'd hate to get you in trouble."

He grinned before heading toward his work shed in the backyard. That left Nick on his own with Julia, which was awkward. He hadn't planned on seeing her again, so he hadn't both-ered to apologize for his poor behavior yesterday. Another strike against him. Considering his dis-mal track record with women, he really should be used to it by now.

Hoping to smooth things over, he motioned her

ahead of him the way he had the first time they met. "Ladies first."

Instead of sailing past him as he'd expected, she studied him for a long, uncomfortable moment. "You're a perplexing man."

Sensing he'd made some progress with her, he grinned back. "I've been called worse."

To his immense relief, she laughed. Shaking her head, she added, "I can only imagine."

When she turned up the snow-covered walkway, her foot slipped, and she nearly went down on the gravel. Nick reached out to catch her, and by some bizarre happening she ended up in his arms.

Holding her lightly, he gazed down into those sparkling blue eyes. Wearing her ivory coat and framed by the white snow, she reminded him of the Victorian angel ornament that had reigned over the top of his mother's Christmas tree since he was a little boy. Elegant and beautiful, with the wispy look of something that might vanish into thin air if he closed his eyes.

Part of him longed to maintain that hold, to keep her close and enjoy the scent of magnolias that followed her everywhere. Instead, he did the gentlemanly thing and released her.

"It's a little slippery," he managed to say as he took her arm and guided her to a clear section of the path. "Watch your step."

She rewarded him with a queenly smile. "I will. Thank you."

While he stood there watching her go up the path, he noticed the very distinctive way she moved. With the grace of a ballerina, she seemed to float over the snow, barely touching the ground before going up the steps. Nick had dated plenty of models and dancers, but he'd never met a woman who walked the way Julia did.

People didn't usually snare his attention this quickly, but she'd managed it somehow. It was a good thing he was headed back to Richmond tomorrow, or he might have given in to his curiosity and done something stupid like ask her to dinner.

Right, he thought with a grimace, as if there was any chance of her saying yes, whether he stayed in town or not. Men had probably taken her to Paris for dinner and a ride on the Seine. There was no way a guy like him could compete with that, even if he wanted to. Which he didn't.

Unfortunately, a tiny, annoying part of him disagreed, and he was wrestling it back into submission when Todd jogged up and stopped beside him. "Coming?"

"In a minute."

Todd gave him a curious look but shrugged and followed Julia into the house. Standing there with snow falling all around him, Nick took a deep, chilly breath of air. He'd never met a woman who rattled him as thoroughly as Julia Stanton did. Whether that was good or bad, he couldn't say.

But it was definitely interesting.

When Nick came through the door into the cozy kitchen, Julia watched as his niece attacked him like a frenzied cub.

"We're doing the tree today!" she shouted with obvious joy. "That means you can help us."

"I don't know about all that," he hedged, hanging his coat on the rack near the door. "I'm not much use in the decorating department."

"Oh, it's easy," Todd assured him between sips of cocoa. "Just do what the girls tell you, and you'll be fine."

Taking a steaming reindeer mug from Lainie, Nick chuckled. "This might come as a shock, but I'm not in the habit of taking orders from anyone."

He sat down, and instantly Hannah was in his lap. Having seen him at his prickly worst, Julia thought it was adorable how his niece had taken to her brusque uncle.

"What do you do at your house for Christmas, Uncle Nick?" Hannah asked.

"I pretty much hang a wreath on the door and call it done. I don't have kids, so it's not a big deal."

"Julia doesn't have kids, either," Lainie pointed out. "And she does a fabulous job with her decorations."

"She sure does." He flashed her an approving grin that actually made her blush. To hide her reaction, she lifted her Frosty the Snowman mug for a sip of cocoa.

"You need somewhere to put your angel," Hannah informed him in a very grown-up voice. "Ours came from Eye-land."

"Ireland," her mother corrected her. "Gramma brought it back from one of her trips to Waterford."

Hannah looked up at Nick with wide eyes. "Did she bring you one, too?"

Nick traded an uncomfortable look with Lainie but finally nodded. "It's different from yours, but it's really pretty. I keep it on a shelf in my living room, and whenever I look at it, it reminds me of Gramma."

The kitchen went silent, and Julia could hear the quiet ticking of the mantel clock in the next room. A quick glance at Lainie told Julia her friend wasn't accustomed to her tightly controlled brother opening up that way. Then again, you'd need a heart of stone to resist Hannah Martin's innocent charm.

"That's nice," she rattled on, "but we put ours

on the tree. Daddy usually lifts me up to set her on, but since you're here you could do it."

Clearly worn down, Nick gave in with a chuckle. "Sure, munchkin. I'll give you a hand."

"Yay!" Now she turned pleading eyes on Julia. "Can you help us? You're so good with ribbons and stuff."

This time, she didn't check her watch. It simply wasn't in her to disappoint any child, but especially not this one. A few months ago, she'd hesitantly entered the Safe Harbor Church for the first time and searched for a place to sit in the crowded chapel. Lainie Martin had spotted her and slid down to make room for the new girl in town.

That simple, friendly gesture marked the beginning of a solid friendship Julia had come to treasure, and she was touched that they'd include her in one of their family traditions. "I'd love to, Hannah. Thank you for asking."

After hugging Nick and then Julia, she scampered away with her parents to start gathering up the ornaments.

"She's such a doll," Julia said as she took a seat across the table from Nick. "You must love her to pieces."

"It's hard not to."

The wistfulness in his tone alerted her that something was bothering him. While she suspected what it might be, she thought it might help him to voice it out loud—with a little nudging from her along the way. "It's nice to be with family this time of year, isn't it?"

"Yeah." Looking down at his hands, he wove his fingers together before adding, "I've missed a lot the past few years."

"You're here now."

When he lifted his eyes to hers, the misery in them made her want to give him a hug. She still thought it would help him to talk out what he was feeling, but she couldn't bring herself to press on still-aching wounds. Old hurts were the worst, she knew, and some never healed. She had no idea what had estranged him from his family, but for Nick's sake, she decided it was best to change the subject. "When did you last go sledding?"

Her question had the desired effect, and his expression brightened as he laughed. "Ten years ago, maybe more."

"If this snow keeps up, we'll be able to do something about that. There's a great hill at the edge of town."

"Spinnaker Hill, out near the old saw mill," he filled in. "Cooper Landry and I used to ice down a track and race the other guys after school."

"That's right. Bree told me you and Cooper were friends growing up." Julia had a hard time imagining this hard-driving man hanging out with Holiday Harbor's easygoing mayor for more than five minutes, but odder things had happened.

"Best friends," Nick confirmed. "He was why I sent Bree to do those stories over the summer. The original article was Cooper's idea. It started as a puff piece to lure in some tourists and ended up exposing some honest-to-goodness corporate fraud."

"A juicy story like that must be good for your magazine."

He flashed her another version of that nearly irresistible grin. "We won a few awards for bold journalism, if that's what you mean. Readers love that kind of stuff, 'cause it reminds them of what could happen in their own backyards."

"And that sells subscriptions."

His grin faded considerably. "Not as many as I'd like, and building up subscriptions is a constant headache. To be honest, I'm jealous of Bree, getting to sniff out a story and set it up for people to read. Designing layouts and keeping up with invoices aren't nearly as much fun as writing."

"I know what you mean," Julia sympathized. "I love stocking and arranging the store and working with customers. When it comes to the bookwork, though, it's like torture."

"I'm curious about something." She motioned for him to continue, and he asked, "Of all the things you could do, why a toy store?"

No one but her parents had ever asked her that, mostly because few people knew where she was and what she was currently doing. Now that she thought about it, maybe that was one reason the locals had been so slow to warm up to her. They simply didn't understand why she was there in the first place.

To Nick, she said, "I earned a degree in Business and International Relations by taking classes wherever my parents were living at the time. I've always enjoyed collecting toys, so when I decided to move here, opening a toy store seemed like a good way to blend my hobby with my education."

"It can't be easy in this economy."

"Neither is running an online magazine," she pointed out, "but like you, I do my best to offer people something unique they can't get anywhere else."

She appreciated that he didn't question why on earth someone from such a wealthy background was working at all. That was something she'd rather not discuss with anyone if she could possibly help it.

"Sounds like we've got something in common after all," he commented lightly.

"What's that?"

"We're both masochists who'd rather work 24/7 and be in charge of our own business than put in forty hours a week for someone else."

Julia didn't think of it that way. Her mother had set aside her own dreams to marry the love of her life and accompany him around the world. While she seemed content with her choice, Julia treasured her hard-won independence and would never sacrifice it again.

Caught up in her thoughts, she'd missed what Nick was saying. Embarrassment warmed her cheeks, and she smiled. "I'm sorry. What were you saying?"

"I was saying I can't believe you like to sled."

"And snowmobile and ski. I took some snowboarding lessons in Gstaad last winter, but it's harder than it looks."

Too late, she realized he might interpret that as bragging. Because of the exotic life she'd led, people often jumped to conclusions about her, and she'd learned to keep her adventures under wraps. Fortunately, he seemed to take it in stride. "The Swiss Alps, huh? Didn't peg you for a snow bunny."

"What? You thought I was the kind of girl who dresses the part and then holes up in the lodge with a warm drink, watching everyone else have all the fun?"

After a few moments, he grinned. "Guess so."

"The media only sees what I want them to see," she informed him coolly. "That means there's a lot about me you don't know."

"Is that right?" The teasing glint left his eyes, and as he leaned forward, they simmered with an enticing combination of challenge and fascination. "You mean, like why a classy, sophisticated woman like you is hiding out in a backwoods place like this?"

"I'm not hiding." When he tilted his head in a chiding gesture, she hedged. "Not exactly. I just wanted a fresh start, and this seemed like a good place to do it."

He smirked. "Nice try, cupcake, but I'm not buying it."

Somehow, they'd slid into dangerous territory, and she instinctively pulled away from the edge. Painful as the lessons were, Julia had learned a lot from the scam artist who'd gone to great trouble to win her affection, only to reveal his motives had nothing to do with love. She'd made the mistake of trusting him too fully, and it had cost her more than she was willing to risk ever again.

The man sitting across the table, with his dark good looks and complex personality, intrigued her in much the same way. It was a screaming red flag for her. In her memory, she heard her father's common-sense advice.

You never know what a man's thinking, Julia. His actions speak the truth, even if he's lying through his teeth.

Recognizing the male interest in Nick's eyes,

she resisted the impulse to duck her head and murmur something demure. All her life she'd done the proper thing, and it had brought her more heartache than she cared to recall. Moving here had enabled her to start becoming her own person, far from the refined stage she'd played on for so many years.

This time, she held her head high and met his smoldering gaze with a fearless one of her own. "This may come as a surprise to you, but I don't really care what you believe."

Before she could say anything more, her phone pinged with a text all in capital letters. *SOS— COMPUTER CRASHED*.

Grateful for an excuse to leave the too-intriguing journalist behind, she made her apologies to the Martins and drove back to Toyland.

When Julia's assistant called her away, Nick fought the urge to walk her out. This wasn't his house, he reasoned, so it wasn't his place to do it anyway. Instead, he nodded goodbye and pretended to be engrossed in the knotted lights Todd had just handed him.

The truth was, her blatant rejection still stung.

One minute they were bantering back and forth, and the next she morphed into the Ice Queen. Maybe being called a snow bunny annoyed her, he thought, taking the lights into the living room where Lainie and Hannah were unloading ornaments from a box.

One thing he knew for certain: it didn't matter if she liked him or despised him. Tomorrow morning, he'd be leaving Holiday Harbor—and its puzzling new resident—and heading back to warm, sunny Richmond. He'd been so cold the past few days, it would probably take him a week to completely thaw out.

"Brrr," Todd commented, echoing Nick's thoughts while unloading an armload of wood. "The temperature's really dropping out there."

As he tossed logs onto the fire, Noah bounced in a swing that hung from the door frame, gurgling his baby opinion. With Christmas carols playing on the stereo and Hannah chirping about the history of this ornament and that one, the Martins' modest living room hummed like a restless beehive.

As if on cue, Lainie came over to sit on the threadbare arm of Nick's chair. "Nice, huh?"

"Sure, if you like that gooey family thing."

Laughing, she gave him a playful smack on the shoulder. "If you hate it so much, why don't you hide up in the guest room?"

"It's warmer down here," he retorted.

"Oh, come on. This has to be better than an empty condo with a wreath on the door."

"Sure," he grumbled, "'til you have to clean it all up."

"That's my big brother, always finding the clouds," she said matter-of-factly. "You're s-o-o serious about everything, I don't know how you stand it."

He couldn't, Nick nearly blurted but managed to stop himself. After their earlier tiff about Ian, he didn't want to bring up the past again. Lainie was three years younger than him but had grown up considerably since becoming a mom. At her prodding, Nick had endured some long, painful talks this week, and they'd begun rebuilding the once-close relationship he'd destroyed when he all but disappeared from her life. He figured the best way to keep that going was to leave the past buried and move on.

Lainie picked up a needle and started threading it through fresh popcorn. It smelled too good to resist, and Nick snuck a few pieces when she wasn't looking. Her nonstop chattering about people around town alerted Nick that something was on her mind, and he grinned. Some things never changed. "What is it, Lain?"

Keeping her eyes on what she was doing, she said, "We'll be going to a special service tonight. You're welcome to come with us if you want."

Nick hadn't voluntarily attended church since he was eight. With the exception of Lainie and

Todd's wedding, he hadn't seen the inside of one in more than ten years. And even if he was suffering from an attack of remorse and mistakenly entered a sanctuary, it certainly wouldn't be his father's.

He gave his sister a chiding look which she didn't notice because she refused to meet his gaze. To avoid upsetting Hannah, he softly said, "You know me better than that."

Her careless shrug did nothing to hide her disappointment. "I thought it was worth a try. People change."

"Not me," he assured her as gently as he could. "I made that decision a long time ago for lots of reasons. It's the way I've chosen to live my life, and I'm good with it."

Letting the popcorn strand fall into the bowl, she looked at him with pleading eyes. "I don't understand why you insist on doing everything the hardest way possible. Todd and I get so much from our faith and that really helps when things get tough. Like when he lost his teaching job here, and Hannah was so sick. It was the worst time to have another baby, and when we found out about Noah, it felt like a disaster. God led us through all that. Todd found an even better position in Oakbridge, and we've never been happier."

When she finally paused for a breath, Nick couldn't help smiling up at her. She was so sweet, crediting God for something she and Todd had accomplished through determination and hard work. Taking her hand, he said, "I'm glad to hear that, but it doesn't work that way for everyone. Some of us are outside the circle, and there's nothing we can do about it."

"That's not true," she whispered intently, squeezing his hand between both of hers. "I know it's not. God hasn't forgotten about you, Nick. You just have to open up and let Him back into your life."

She couldn't be more wrong, but he didn't want to debate religion with her while her husband and daughter were arranging figurines of Jesus and the wise men in the manger on a nearby table.

So, out of respect for his sister and her happy family, Nick swallowed his pride and kept his mouth shut.

Early Monday morning, Nick found himself back at Toyland, drinking the best coffee he'd had in days while Julia laid out the unexpected offer she'd hinted at on the phone last night. He couldn't believe his ears.

"An exclusive?" he echoed, getting a nod in reply. Sitting by the lobby fireplace in a burgundy velvet wing chair, he was surrounded by more Christmas trappings than he'd ever seen in his life. It was enough to make him wonder if he was losing his grip on reality. "I thought you wanted to keep your new life here a secret."

"Oh, that couldn't last." Flicking her hand in a queenly gesture, she set off a string of silver jingle bells divided by what he assumed were tiny sapphires. Lots of them. "Some reporter or another will track me down eventually. This way, I control the situation."

"And the message," he added, to show he understood. "In case you haven't figured it out already, I'm not used to taking orders. What makes you think I'll play along?"

Leaning forward, she pinned him with a knowing look. "Yesterday, you told me you miss getting the scoop and writing your own stories. I'm giving you one, right here, right now. Take it or leave it."

Ordinarily he wasn't a fan of ultimatums, but he was tempted beyond belief. Nick didn't doubt for a second that if he didn't grab this opportunity, another journalist would. Julia's story had flash and grit, two things people loved to read about. The businessman in him immediately went into promotional gear, considering the impact something like this might have. New *Kaleidoscope* readers could sample this rich-and-famous storyline, then purchase a limited subscription to read the ending. If things worked out, they'd like what they saw and buy a full subscription. Since he'd be doing the work, there'd be no freelance writer to pay so everything that came in would be pure profit. Unlike most business arrangements he made, there was no downside for him.

Of course, agreeing to her terms meant he'd be stuck in Holiday Harbor longer than he'd planned. But because everything was handled online, he could run the magazine from anywhere. It was something he'd never taken advantage of before, aside from using his condo's spare room as an office. But for a story like this, it might make sense to change things up, even if it meant staying in the last place he wanted to be. In the overall scheme of things, the impact such a high-profile article would have on his business was worth a little discomfort. Beyond that, he'd be writing again. Researching Julia would be interesting enough. Getting to know the reclusive ambassador's daughter through personal interviews would be downright fascinating. "One thing."

"Yes?"

"You've had an amazing life, along with your parents. I don't think one article will do it justice."

For a split second, he thought he saw a smile quivering at the corner of her mouth. Then it was gone, and she asked, "What do you have in mind?"

"A serialized biography, book-length, but posted online in pieces." Inspiration struck, and he added, "We'll call the new section 'Person of Interest.' Readers will get hooked and come back every week for the latest segment on the extraordinary Julia Stanton."

"So this will help your business?"

"Definitely. Yours, too. Once folks know you're here, your online orders should go through the roof."

"I hadn't thought of that. It would be nice to do my books with black ink instead of red."

The way she said it convinced him she was being totally honest with him—she really hadn't considered the financial benefit that would come from the articles. Nick couldn't imagine why else she'd propose an invasion of her self-imposed exile, but maybe by the time they were done, it would make sense to him.

For now, he scoffed, "Like that's a problem for you."

That got him a steely glare. "Rule number one—assume nothing. Things in my life aren't always what they seem to be."

Picking up on her somber tone, he nodded. "Got it. Does that mean I'm in?"

When she offered him a slender hand to seal their deal, it occurred to him this was the first time he'd allowed a woman to call the shots with him. Why Julia was so different, he couldn't say, but it added another angle to their—friendship?

No, that wasn't right. He'd just met her, and they'd spent most of their time dancing around the ring, trying to get a read on each other.

He couldn't say where all that posturing might lead, but he sure was looking forward to finding out.

Chapter Four

"I won't be opening the store for another hour," Julia said as she stood. To her surprise, Nick got to his feet in a gentlemanly gesture she hadn't expected. Apparently, his manners were better than he'd led her to believe. "Would you like a tour of the building?"

"Sure."

He'd already seen her office, and he politely followed her through the storeroom, piled high with boxes of toys she had to inventory before restocking the shelves. He didn't pose many questions or take notes, instead letting her ramble on about whatever she thought might be most interesting to him. When he asked how she decided how much of each thing to buy, she laughed.

"Most people drop dead of boredom by this point," she said approvingly. "You're very patient."

"This was your idea, not mine," he pointed out. "I don't wanna push."

"Is that right?" Folding her arms, she gazed at him thoughtfully. "From what I've seen, *Kaleidoscope* doesn't pull punches with other sources. What makes me so different?"

"You tell me."

A lazy grin moved across his features, settling in to gleam in his dark eyes. It was a challenging look, as if he'd stumbled across a mystery that fascinated him. Realizing *she* was that mystery made her flush and take a hesitant step back. With his brooding poet looks and dangerous vibe, Nick McHenry was just the kind of man she was drawn to.

And just the kind of man she needed to avoid.

Reminding herself that their current arrangement was really aimed at making peace between him and his father, she quickly regained her composure and smiled. "Maybe you'll find some answers upstairs."

Turning, she led him to a door marked PRIVATE. Just as he had the morning they met, he reached past her to open it. "Ladies first."

On her way up, she flicked on a light switch and was greeted with a loud, "When shall we three meet again, in thunder, lightning, or in rain?"

The two phrases rhymed perfectly in a highbrow British accent, and Nick stopped dead, cocking his head with a baffled expression. "What was that?"

"Shakespeare."

"I recognize the line from *Hamlet,* but who said it?"

"Shakespeare," she repeated, continuing up the creaky wooden steps. "Come on and I'll introduce you."

"O-kay."

He dragged the word out in a doubtful tone, and she allowed herself a little smile. It was nice to know she could knock him off balance the way he'd done to her. After her disastrous last relationship, being on even footing with Nick made her feel more confident than she had in months.

The large room mirrored the one downstairs with one exception: it was almost completely unfurnished. The only things she had up here were a few pieces of furniture and the built-in bookshelves full of treasures from all around the world. Ignoring Nick's shocked look, she strolled to a wooden rod that stretched the width of the generous bay window overlooking Main Street.

Perched there was an enormous blue-and-yellow macaw who eyed her with what could only be described as fondness. Bobbing his head, he croaked, "Good morn to you, milady."

"And to you, sir."

"Oh, man," Nick muttered from a safe distance. "Does that parrot have an English accent?"

"Actually, he's a macaw with a Welsh accent." Julia pushed up the sleeve of her sweater, and the bird stepped elegantly onto her arm. "He's from Cardiff."

The stately bird focused intelligent black eyes on Nick and bobbed his head again. "Greetings to you, sir."

"Back at ya."

Grinning, Nick joined them by the window. When he picked up a piece of dried fruit and offered it to Shakespeare, the bird replied with something between a cluck and a whistle. "Many thanks."

While he munched his treat, Nick ran a fingertip over a brightly colored wing. "How'd you end up with this charmer?"

"My friend Liam is abroad on a six-month assignment and couldn't take Shakespeare with him. We've always gotten along well, so he's staying with me. It's been fun, hasn't it?" She tickled under his chin, and the bird winked at her.

"Ah, Julia, shall I compare thee to a summer's day?" he cooed, affectionately rubbing his long comb of feathers against her hand.

That got Nick's attention, and he gave her a knowing look. "Good ol' Liam taught him to say that, didn't he?"

"Well, yes," she stammered, feeling herself growing pink again.

"And he left his bard-quoting buddy with you so you wouldn't forget about him while he's away."

"I suppose."

"And eventually, you'll have to get together so you can give him his bird back," Nick continued in the cynical, hard-edged tone she'd heard too often from him. "Clever."

Say something, she scolded herself. *Tell him he's got it all wrong.*

Carefully setting Shakespeare back on his perch, she began, "It's not like that at all."

"So you don't love him back?"

"Of course not. We're friends, and I'm pet sitting—simple as that."

Stepping closer, Nick fixed her with an unreadable look. "In my experience, nothing between a man and a woman is ever simple."

Ordinarily, she wouldn't engage a near-stranger in a debate over personal relationships. But for this man, with his cool demeanor and jaded attitude, she decided to make an exception.

Facing him squarely, she returned his glare with one of her own. "I have no doubt you're very good at seeing the worst in people. It probably serves you well in your line of work but I have news for you. I'm not like most people you've met, and your cynic's routine won't work on me."

"Is that right?" He didn't come any closer, but even from a distance, it was obvious she had his full attention. "What makes you so different?"

Refusing to back away even a single inch, she held out her arms. "All this makes me different. If you really want to know more about me, take a look at what I've chosen to surround myself with."

His eyes held hers, and she got the distinct impression he was trying to read her. Too bad for him, since she'd learned long ago to mask her true feelings with a cloak of impeccable manners. When he finally spoke, his voice was hardly above a murmur.

"Where is everything?"

Jolted by the bizarre question, she fought the urge to avert her gaze and back away. The tone in his voice sounded almost sympathetic, as if he'd somehow discovered the secret she'd been keeping for nearly a year. Accustomed to intrusive queries, fending them off had become second nature to her. But now she found herself at a complete loss for words.

What on earth was wrong with her?

"What do you mean?" she demanded, firming her chin with determination. "I'm not sure what you were expecting, but this is all I have."

Shaking his head, he said, "All you *still* have. What happened to the rest?"

"I sold some of my collection to start my business."

Folding his arms, he pinned her with a knowing look. "You expect me to believe you never owned full-size versions of all those pieces of doll house luxury you've got in miniature downstairs?"

Julia opened her mouth to object but quickly realized any protest she might offer would be a blatant lie. The trouble was, she knew the truth would be fodder for the serialized version of her life story he wanted to write. So she chose her words carefully. "I had some financial problems."

"Which is why you dropped out of sight." When she nodded, he prodded, "You don't strike me as the type to gamble or waste money. What did you fall into?"

"Love." Hoping to escape the laser focus of those dark, intelligent eyes, she busied herself filling Shakespeare's water bottle. "In a nutshell, Bernard wasn't the man I thought he was. By the time I figured out what was going on, he'd used what he knew about me to steal my identity. And most of my money," she added with a grimace.

Nick hissed something nasty under his breath, but she ignored it while she changed out the newspapers under the macaw's open perch. "Where were the police in all this?"

"Helpless." Swallowing hard, Julia turned to face him. "I met him in Switzerland, where he was a banker. Using their confidential system and my personal information, he transferred out what he wanted and disappeared."

"What about your father's connections?" Nick asked angrily. "He must know people all over the world."

"When a clever person has enough money, he can hide from even the best investigators. It's not easy, but if you know how, it can be done. With his banking background, he knew exactly what he was doing. After six months of humiliation and dead ends, I ended the investigation so I could get on with my life." Glancing around, she let the past go and smiled proudly. "I sold what I could, and my parents loaned me the rest so I could start over. Once Toyland is profitable, I'll pay them back as quickly as I can."

"I'm surprised they didn't just give you the money."

"They wanted to, but I wouldn't let them." The words came out more easily now. She'd never shared her mortifying personal history with anyone, and she'd feared that confiding it to him would make her feel awful. His nonjudgmental response to it was a nice boost to her confidence, encouraging her to continue. "All my life, I've been viewed like a princess—pleasant company but not much else. I'm capable of a lot more than that, and I intend to prove it."

The rigid lines of his face mellowed into something she hadn't expected to see from him: respect. "I think you're on the right track with that. I'm as cynical as they come, and you've already convinced me."

Unexpected, the warmth of his praise made her blush, and she angled her face away to hide her reaction from him. "Thank you." After a beat of silence, she forced herself to step away. "I usually have new orders coming in by now, so I should check my email. You're welcome to have a look around."

With that, she left him standing in the middle of her cavernous living room and headed down the short hall to her study. She sensed him watching her, and she fought off the impulse to look back. It would make her look foolish, and after confiding her embarrassing past to him, that was the last thing she wanted right now.

Behind her, Shakespeare crooned, "Alas, fair maiden! Parting is such sweet sorrow."

She was accustomed to the bird's extensive Elizabethan repertoire, and she barely registered the poetic farewell. But when she heard Nick laugh and quote the next line, she allowed herself a little smile.

It was a huge risk, opening up to him the way

she did, but Nick had taken it well. Now that she'd glimpsed a softer side of the gruff journalist, the prospect of getting to know him was beginning to appeal to her.

Nick watched her go because he couldn't help it.

Julia seemed to have the kind of innate grace he'd rarely seen outside of movie stars. Normally a down-to-earth kind of guy, he kept getting the feeling that she'd stepped out of the pages of some old Gothic novel, sweeping down the staircase to greet her visitors and welcome them to her palatial home.

Only this wasn't the right setting, and he frowned at the nearly empty space he was standing in. An oversize chair and sofa sat in the corner near Shakespeare's domain, opposite a coffee table and buffet that held a small flat-screen TV. Granted, the carved tables looked like antiques, and the leather upholstery felt as smooth and rich as butter, but other than that, there was nothing. Except for the most eclectic assortment of objects he'd ever seen.

African masks and dainty statues of ballerinas were mixed in among things he couldn't even come close to identifying. In its paws, a stuffed koala held a frame with a picture of a younger Julia cuddling the real thing, and he smiled as he recalled her telling him about the furry orphan. More photos were tucked in here and there, but the most impressive part of her collection was on the other side of the room.

Books. Hundreds of them, first and second editions, in English, Italian, French, Greek, even a few in Russian. Shelved alphabetically by author, they represented the best classical literature ever published. There'd been a time when he'd hoped to join these authors, his heroes, on the shelves of people smart enough to appreciate great writing when they saw it. Unfortunately in college he'd discovered that his hard-hitting style was better suited to reality than fiction. But standing here, facing the authors who'd inspired the dream he'd put away years ago, made him wish he'd kept trying.

If wishes were horses, beggars would ride.

His father's pragmatic New England wisdom echoed in Nick's memory, dragging him back to reality. He was a reporter, here to do a story on a captivating woman who'd basically given him carte blanche to investigate her life. It was time he got to work.

He could still hear her tapping away on her computer, so he decided it was okay to do a little digging. Scanning the titles, he found one of his favorites and slipped a copy of *A Christmas Carol* from its spot. He opened the cover, and his jaw fell open as he read the inscription scrawled on the embossed bookmark.

For Julia, a fellow lover of Dickens who would have charmed Scrooge himself.

It was signed by the Prime Minister of England.

Whoa. Very carefully, Nick closed the book and slid it back into place. A spot check of the others showed the majority of them were gifts, mostly from men. While he wasn't surprised to discover she had a horde of admirers, it did bother him. Why, he couldn't say, and he pushed the puzzling reaction aside when he heard her footsteps in the hallway.

"See anything that interests you?" she asked, nodding toward her impressive library.

The woman standing in front of him interested him very much, but Nick opted not to share that just yet. After their very personal conversation earlier, he didn't want to do or say anything that might make her feel pressured. The last man she'd had faith in had betrayed her in the worst way possible. Nick suspected it would take some time to convince her that—although male—he could be trusted.

"It's quite a collection, that's for sure. You can read all these languages?"

She laughed. "Hebrew and Japanese aren't in my repertoire, but I'm solid with the others. When you travel as much as I do, it really helps to know several languages. What about you?"

"Some high school Spanish, but that's it." He glanced around with a sigh. "I've always wanted to travel, though."

"Why haven't you?"

Her simple question made him wonder why, too, and he shrugged. "Never got around to it, I guess. Getting away from here was enough."

"Nick?" The gentle tone got his attention, and he turned to face her. "What happened between you and your father?"

Every muscle in his body tensed, and he scowled. "That's none of your business."

She never even blinked. She was either the bravest woman he'd ever met or the most foolish. "I trusted you with the truth about myself," she reminded him calmly, settling on the arm of the only chair in the room. "You can do the same with me. I promise."

"I don't think so."

"It's obvious something awful happened to your family. I'm not asking to be nosy—I'm asking because I want to help. They all went out of their way to make me feel at home when I moved here, and I've come to love them very much. They're fantastic people, and I can't imagine what could be so terrible that you'd cut yourself off from them for so long."

No one invaded his privacy this way, and for good reason. If they dared to try, he'd deliver a parting blow and storm out, slamming a door behind him for good measure. For some reason, he stood his ground with Julia, though he was glowering for all he was worth. "Maybe I'm not so wonderful. Did you consider that?"

"Not for a second. Lainie wouldn't love you the way she does if you were anything less than wonderful."

Mesmerized by those sparkling blue eyes and the soothing lilt of her voice, he heard himself say, "It's a long, sad story."

"I have time."

She didn't even glance at her watch, and he was reminded of how she'd ignored the time when Hannah had asked her to stay. Accustomed to racing from one deadline to the next, that attitude was totally foreign to him. "Don't you have to open your store?"

She waved that concern away in the regal gesture that seemed to be part of her personality. Great, he thought with a mental groan. He'd just met the woman, and already he was memorizing her quirks. That didn't bode well for his sanity during this assignment.

"One nice thing about doing business in Holiday Harbor—a half-hour doesn't make much difference one way or another. Would you like some more coffee?"

"Sure. Thanks."

As he made himself comfortable on the sofa, Nick recognized that she'd picked up on his nerves and was offering him a chance to pull himself together. Not to back out of 'fessing up, though. Generous but tough, he mused with a grin. In his experience, most people were one or the other, and he'd never thought to find that unusual combination in such a gorgeous woman. Just one more thing that made her stand out among all the others he'd known.

Shakespeare edged down his pole, stopping near Nick's seat. Tilting his feathered head, he gave Nick an unsettlingly intelligent look. "All the world's a stage, and all the men and women merely players."

In spite of himself, Nick laughed. "Dude, you have no idea."

"I'm glad you two are getting along," Julia said as she came in carrying a tray with two steaming mugs and a carafe of the most delicious coffee he'd ever smelled. "It didn't take me long to discover the Bard isn't fond of men in general."

"Kind of a watch bird, huh?" Nick picked up his mug and inhaled the heady scent of a tropical island. The smell alone was enough to get his brain in gear, and he asked, "What is this stuff? And how'd you find it way up here?"

"It's a Kona blend. I occasionally buy a bag of it from Amelia Landry when I'm at her bookstore, but she won't tell me where she gets it. Even Bree and Cooper don't know, but it goes really well with gingerbread."

After a long sip, he commented, "Not a fan of gingerbread myself."

"Ah, yes," she said, leaning back in her chair to cross one slender leg over the other. It was a classic film-star pose but one that looked completely natural on her. "One more reason for hating Christmas. You were going to tell me how all that came about."

Actually, he'd rather take a header off the town's famous Last Chance Lighthouse into the icy ocean. Admitting that would sound pathetic, though, so he swallowed another mouthful of coffee and retreated back into his painful past. "You probably don't know I was the middle child in our family. Our brother, Ian, was three years older than me and he was just about perfect. Even when we were kids, he knew he wanted to be a preacher."

When he paused, Julia smiled encouragement. "Like your father."

"Yeah. Anyway, one day we were out fishing, and we started messing around in the boat. Trying to knock each other off into the water with the oars—you know how kids do." Pausing again, he took a deep breath and stared down at the mug in his hands. "I came in too hard, and Ian went flying out. He stayed down a long time, but I didn't think anything of it. He used to fool around like that, trying to scare me, so I figured he was doing it again." Out of pure, stubborn pride, he met her gaze. "He never came back up."

"Oh, Nick," she whispered, sympathy shining in her beautiful eyes.

"When I realized something was wrong, I dove in and found him near some rocks we hadn't known about. I pulled him out, but it was too late. The sheriff figured Ian hit his head when he fell and drowned within a minute."

"How old were you?"

"Twelve. Ian was our father's favorite, then and now, and Dad never let me forget it. No matter what I did, I could never live up to what he wanted because I wasn't Ian. Finally, I gave up trying and went the opposite way of everything he ever taught us. Somehow, it seemed easier that way," he added quietly.

When she didn't respond, he looked up to find her studying him with a pensive expression. He didn't like the feeling it gave him, and he braced himself for whatever she was about to say.

"Are you saying your father blames you for Ian's death?"

"Why wouldn't he? It was my fault." Nick made it a point not to think about it too much because every time he did, his heart twisted with fresh grief for the tragedy that had scarred his family. The fact that it could have been avoided only made him feel worse, and although he'd accepted long ago that he couldn't change the past, he wished there was some way to lock it away and destroy the key.

Without asking, Julia refilled his mug. "I'm sure Ann and Lainie don't feel that way. Awful as it was, what happened was an accident. You didn't mean to hurt your brother."

"I did worse than hurt him," Nick insisted, leaning in to make her understand. "Me being stupid cost Ian his life, and my family lost everything he could've been. He was smart and funny, and he really cared about people, even at that age. When Dad retired, Ian would've taken over the church and kept it all going. When he died, everything changed."

"For you, too," she reminded him gently. "You've spent most of your life trying to escape it. Now I understand why you moved so far away. It wasn't the weather or the size of the town—it was the memories."

"I never should've let Lainie talk me into coming home. It was a huge mistake." Julia held his gaze for several long, uncomfortable moments. When a faint smile lifted the corner of her mouth, he asked, "What?"

"You said 'coming home,' not 'coming back.' Does that mean you still consider Holiday Harbor your home?"

This classy lady was a lot sharper than he'd given her credit for, and Nick fought the urge to squirm like a kid caught breaking the rules. Kind but firm, she'd somehow managed to skirt his usual defenses and get to the core of what made him tick. No woman had ever upended him that way, and he wasn't crazy about it. "I don't get attached to places the way other people do. Give me a laptop and a wireless connection, and I'm good to go."

"Interesting, but you didn't answer my question."

Nick brushed off her observation with a short laugh. "I thought *I* was supposed to be interviewing *you*."

"True, but while you're doing that, we're bound to learn a few things about each other."

There was an intriguing twinkle in her eyes he hadn't noticed before, and Nick took that as an encouraging sign that she was warming up to him. With most people, he knew more than he wanted to within minutes of meeting them. But the more he learned about Julia, the more he wanted to know. "You mean, like friends do?"

Her smile warmed. "Just like that. We're about as different as two people can be, but with a little effort, I think we could be great friends."

Nick watched her thoughtfully as she stood and picked up the tray to take it back into the kitchen. He didn't usually make a habit of singling out a particular woman to spend his time with, and the thought of doing it now rattled him. He dated when he had the chance, but he never got involved. It was too much work, he'd always told himself, and having a girlfriend required more of his energy than he cared to give.

While that strategy had stood him well through the years, he couldn't shake the impression that Julia was different. Remarkable as she was, a woman like her just might be worth the risk.

For some other man—someone without a train wreck for a past. Someone who could give her a solid and certain future. Not for him.

Later that week, the bells on Toyland's front door jingled, and Julia looked up to find Mavis Freeman striding into her shop. The keeper of Holiday Harbor's famous lighthouse, Mavis was notorious for her crusty demeanor and sharp tongue. But to the right people, she allowed a glimpse of a good heart. Julia was fortunate enough to be one of those people.

Coming around the counter, she greeted her visitor warmly. "Good morning, Mavis. How are things out on the point?"

"Drafty and cold," the woman grumbled. "I came into town for a few things and thought I'd stop to see how you're doing with your store."

Julia knew perfectly well no one wanted the honest answer to that, so she replied the way she always did. "Very well, thank you. I've got some fresh goodies from the bakery. Would you like something?"

"Not here for treats." Fishing in the pocket of a heavy man's coat that was much too big for her, the woman took out a crumpled ten dollar bill. "I heard you got a drive going on, to get toys out to young 'uns around town. I can't afford much, but I wanted to bring in something to help 'em have a good Christmas."

"Bless you," Julia said as she took the money. "Every donation is important."

"I don't know what to buy, so I'm hoping you'll take care of that part."

"Of course."

"None o' them half-starved supermodel dolls," Mavis clarified with a scowl. "Go with building blocks or art supplies, something like that."

Julia took the brusque order with a smile. "I

just got in a new shipment, and there are plenty of both."

"Good." Glancing toward the fireplace, the older woman squinted at the table where Nick was tapping away on his laptop. "My eyes ain't what they used to be. Is that Nick McHenry?"

Looking up, he grinned over at her. "Sure is. How're you, Mavis?"

"Well, don't sit over there and make me shout," she scolded. "Come say hello like a normal person."

Julia wouldn't have believed it if she hadn't seen it for herself, but Nick hurried over and gave the bristly keeper a hug. Holding her at arm's length, he asked, "Better?"

"Some." Giving him a stern up-and-down, she harrumphed. "Dressin' kinda fancy these days, aren't you?"

"What? You don't like Italian wool?"

"Good old American wool does fine for most of us," she informed him tartly. "What're you doing here anyway?"

"Writing a series of articles about our local celebrity." Nick traded a glance with Julia, and genuine fondness sparkled in his eyes. Whether it was prompted by Mavis or her, she couldn't be certain, but it was a noticeable change.

"How 'bout that? Is it any good?"

He laughed. "Sunday's intro is free, so you

can read it for yourself and let me know what you think."

"That's a good idea," she approved, "giving folks a taste so they'll come back for more."

"Thanks."

"Well, I'd best let you get back to it," she said before turning to Julia. "Remember what I said about that gift now."

"Building blocks or art supplies."

"Good girl."

Giving them each a short nod, Mavis left the shop as quickly as she'd appeared.

Once she was gone, Nick turned to Julia with an amazed expression. "There are a lot of nuts in this town, but she's the toughest of the bunch. How did you get on her good side so fast?"

"By being patient. Once you get to know her, she's a delightful woman."

"I know, but not many around here take the time to find that out." After a thoughtful look, he added, "I think I underestimated you."

"Don't be too hard on yourself," she said with a laugh. "Most people do."

"By the time I'm done with your biography, they won't make that mistake anymore."

His gaze warmed considerably, and alarm bells started ringing in her head. Hoping to stall any romantic notions that might be forming, she very politely said, "I'll look forward to that."

His shameless grin told her he'd read straight through her tactful response, and it didn't bother him in the least. Fortunately, he didn't say anything more but sauntered back to his workspace and started loading equipment into his bag. "I'm way behind on this week's edition of *Kaleidoscope*. You probably won't see much of me the next few days."

She'd gotten used to him trailing after her, so it would be strange not to connect with him every day. Now that she thought about it, maybe that was for the best. He was very charming when it suited him, and it wouldn't take much effort for her to become attached to him. Since that wasn't part of her carefully orchestrated plan, keeping him at a reasonable distance made sense. To her head anyway.

"All right," she said. "Things will be busy around here, but when you're ready for another interview just let me know."

"Will do."

Shrugging his coat on, he shouldered his leather bag and pulled on his gloves. Then, with a quick wave, he was gone.

After working like a dog to get this week's issue ready, Nick cracked his eyes open Sunday morning, trying to figure out what had woken him up. After a few bleary seconds, the answer hit him: silence. Lainie's house was never quiet, and now it echoed with emptiness. Picking up his phone, he saw it was ten o'clock, which meant everyone was at church and wouldn't be home for a while.

Enjoying the peace, he pulled a pillow up behind him and thumbed into his email. He was even more curious than usual about this week's numbers because his own piece was online. A message from Frankie, *Kaleidoscope*'s IT director, caught his eye.

Stanton idea genius—look at subs!

Nick's pulse shot up the way it had when he first saw his byline in print years ago. Apparently, he wasn't totally jaded yet, he mused with a grin. Reaching for his laptop, he signed into the site's control board and saw that overnight, their subscription rate had zoomed upward like the first rise on a death-defying roller coaster.

The risk he'd taken in offering Julia's intro for free had paid off, big-time, and he breathed an actual sigh of relief. As Mavis had predicted, people were coming back for more on the elusive ambassador's daughter. He wondered if Julia's online orders had gone up the same way his magazine's had.

He scrolled to her number in his contacts list, then stopped short. No doubt she was in church listening to his father's carefully prepared sermon. While she probably silenced her phone during a service, he didn't want to chance interrupting anything important with her Christmas ringtone. He was dying to share his accomplishment with someone, but he settled for thanking Frankie for the news. Then he settled back into bed to savor his victory.

Taking off his editor's hat, he let himself enjoy a more personal satisfaction than he normally got with his business. He usually stood aside and let his reporters take most of the credit for their successes. This time it was his own article that had generated so much interest, and he couldn't remember when he'd last felt so proud of himself.

It never would've happened without Julia, he recognized, and that thought made him smile. The past few days he'd been thinking about her a lot, wondering what she was doing. A few times he'd even wondered if she missed him hanging around her shop. Unless she was the greatest actress in history, she seemed to enjoy his company as much as he enjoyed hers, which wasn't a good idea for either of them. He'd purposefully not called her, hoping some time apart would get her out of his system.

The strategy had always worked before, but he found himself thinking about her even more, looking forward to seeing her again. The harder he tried to focus on other things, the more she kept sneaking into his mind. When he closed his eyes, her face swam into view like a fade-in from a movie. Smiling at him, tilting her head in that chiding gesture that told him she wasn't buying whatever line he'd floated.

Tossing a pillow over his face, Nick groaned. Despite his best efforts, he knew he was way too close to being in serious trouble with the pretty toy store owner. Normally, this would be his cue to move on to someone else or even leave town entirely. But now that he'd started her biography, he couldn't pull the plug without disappointing his readers. Not to mention the fact that once he'd secured the story, he'd promised his mother and sister he'd stay in Holiday Harbor until Christmas. He didn't want to let them down.

That meant he had to do something about his growing attraction to Julia. Since he had no clue what that might be, he decided to sleep on it.

Chapter Five

"Good morning," Julia greeted Nick as she unlocked the door for him on Tuesday. "I was starting to think you'd changed your mind about me."

He gave her an odd look, then shook his head. "Last week was so hectic, I decided to get some business out of the way yesterday so I could focus on your article today."

"The intro was very good," she said, going to the small coffee bar to pour them each a cup. "Did your readers seem to like it?"

"They loved it."

He sipped his coffee, and she waited for him to say something else. When he didn't, she frowned. "You don't look very happy about it, though. Is something wrong?"

That got her a crooked grin. "You're really good at reading people, aren't you?"

"I try to be." Answering a question with a question raised a red flag for her, and she pressed a little. "What is it, Nick?"

After a long, thoughtful look at her, he shook his head again. "Nothing important. Is this a good time for some background on your childhood?"

"As long as I can set up while we chat."

"Works for me."

That was pretty much how the entire day went. When she was between customers, he took the opportunity to ask her questions. When she was busy, he sat at a bistro table near the fireplace and typed away on his computer. It was all very cordial and professional, nothing like their earlier talks.

Which, of course, was exactly how she wanted things to be. She just couldn't pinpoint why it felt so hollow. At six o'clock, she ushered her last customer out and flipped the sign on the door to *Closed*.

When she started flicking off the lights in the rear of the store, Nick looked up with a confused expression. "What're you doing?"

"Closing up so I can get over to the church. They need some more adult help with the Christmas pageant, and I volunteered. Rehearsal is at six-thirty tonight."

"Yeah, I remember those," he commented absently as he resumed typing. "I was always a shepherd."

From his tone, Julia couldn't decide if he considered that a good or bad thing. They hadn't talked about his past at all since he'd dropped his bombshell about his brother, and she'd gone out of her way not to push him to discuss his family any further. He had to be ready before he could truly accept the idea of forgiving himself and making peace with his father. But how could she get him to that point? She'd known dozens of reserved people, but he was the most closed-off soul she'd ever come across. Somehow, she had to figure out a way to get him to be more open with her—and hopefully with his father. Confiding in her had been a good start, but there was still a long way to go.

There were only three weeks left until Christmas and the end of his visit. A tall order, she acknowledged with a sigh, and she still had no clue how to make it happen. Then inspiration struck, and as she turned off the lights on the village tree, she casually asked, "Would you like to come along?"

That got her a short laugh. "No, thanks. Not really my kind of scene."

"Hannah will be there," she prodded while the model train coasted to a stop. "She's playing the lead angel this year, and I'm sure she'd love to show off for her uncle Nick."

That did it. Angling his head, he gave Julia an I-know-what-you're-doing look...but then his shoulders slumped in resignation. "Fine. But I'm officially not a kid person, so I'll only be watching Hannah."

His adorable niece was this Scrooge's weakness and Julia congratulated herself on finding a way to get through his detached facade to the good heart underneath. If only he'd allow more people to see it, his life would be so much easier.

But then he wouldn't be Nick, she reminded herself while she went to get her coat from her office. God had made him the way he was for a reason, and while she didn't understand it, she'd just have to work with what He'd given her. Fortunately, she enjoyed a challenge.

When she came back out front, Nick was ready to go. He held out a hand, and she gave him a puzzled look. "What?"

Shaking his head, he took her coat and made a circular motion with his finger. Coming from him, the gesture stunned her, but she spun around and slid her arms into the sleeves. Her scarf slipped to the floor, and he bent to retrieve it. Gently turning her to face him again, he dangled it around her neck, holding the fringed ends as if he didn't want to let them go.

For a moment, they stood that way, almost touching but not quite. His dark eyes glittered as he stared at her, and awareness danced along every nerve while she waited to see what he'd do next.

Slowly, as if it pained him to do it, he released her scarf and stepped away. "We should get going. You don't want to be late."

More disappointed than she had a right to be, Julia knew if she tried to speak, it would come out in a breathless squeak. Hard as she'd tried to keep him at a distance, nothing had worked. Now she was wishing for him to give her—what? A hug? A kiss? Cautious as she had always been with men, Bernard's betrayal had made her even more so. She must be out of her mind, hoping for such an intimate moment with a man she hardly knew.

Gathering up her dignity, she nodded and headed for the door.

What was he thinking? Nick asked himself while they walked across the square to the church. He'd come dangerously close to kissing Julia just now, and his head was still reeling over the near miss. He'd never been one to pass up a golden opportunity like that before, but those had been with casual acquaintances, women he had no intention of pursuing beyond the occasional dinner out. And this one? he wondered. What did he feel for her? It took less than a second for him to answer his own question, which rattled him even more.

Julia was special.

In the gentle way she spoke, the elegant way she moved, the generous way she lived her life, she was the most amazing woman he'd ever met. And those were only the qualities he could see. Instinct told him if he got to know her better, he'd find even more to admire. If he wasn't careful, she'd become more to him than the fascinating subject of his evolving biography.

And then he'd really be in trouble.

As they approached the chapel, he focused on the snow crunching underfoot to get his thoughts back on an even keel. When he'd agreed to go with her, it hadn't occurred to him that he'd be returning—voluntarily—to a place he'd despised for most of his life. Again, he wondered what was wrong with him.

He didn't realize his feet were dragging until she turned to look back at him. "Are you okay?"

"Sure."

He tried to sound confident, but that familiar feeling of dread started creeping up his spine. Doing his best to shrug it off, he caught up with her in time to open the sanctuary door. Once they were inside, she glanced over her shoulder and turned to him.

Sympathy shone in her eyes, and she murmured, "Nick, if this is too much for you, I understand."

Her unexpected show of kindness was just what

he needed. She was giving him an out, and no one but the two of them would know if he took it. Despite the fact that he barely knew her, he was positive she wouldn't mention it to anyone, not even his sister. Wary by nature, he didn't believe in very many people, and even then it took him a long time. It didn't escape him that this sweet engaging woman had somehow managed to earn his trust without even trying. And while that meant he could trust her not to use this show of weakness against him, it made him not want to disappoint her, either.

"Don't worry about me." Hanging up his coat, he reached out for hers. "I'll sit in the back."

She nearly blasted him off his feet with a brilliant smile. "All the bad boys do."

With that, she spun and left him standing there with his jaw on the floor. Unfortunately, that was how Lainie found him.

"Hey, big brother. You all right?" When he turned to her, she laughed. "Oh, I recognize that. It's the Julia effect."

"She's something else, that's for sure," Nick agreed as he took her and Hannah's coats.

"We love Julia," his niece informed him without hesitation. "Everyone does. Mommy, the other angels are up front. Can I go sit with them?"

The former English teacher cocked her head, and Hannah sighed. "*May* I go sit with them?"

"Yes, you may. I'll be working on costumes in the Sunday school room if you need me."

"Okay."

She took off like a shot, and Lainie ordered, "No running in church."

In response, Hannah skipped toward the altar, and Lainie sighed. "Close enough."

Nick couldn't help laughing. "I like her."

"You would." After seeing her daughter finally sit down in one place, she leveled one of those knowing feminine looks at him. "You like Julia, too."

He shrugged. "From what I hear, everyone does."

"But we've gotten to know her over the past few months. You don't normally warm up to people for years, if ever. What's so different about her?"

"I don't know." On their own, Nick's eyes wandered toward the front of the church where Julia sat cross-legged on the floor and chatted with a group of kids. Hannah was front and center, staring at Julia with heroine-worship in her eyes. He wasn't four, but Nick had a good idea how his niece was feeling right now. "There's something, though. She's not like anyone I've ever met."

"Well, whatever it is, I'm glad." Standing on tiptoe, Lainie kissed his cheek. "I can't remember the last time I saw you look this happy."

She strolled past him to head downstairs, and he stopped her with a hand on her arm. "Have you noticed her hanging out with anyone in particular?" he asked. "Guys, I mean."

Lainie shook her head. "She was with someone last year, in Europe I think. It didn't end well, and all she'll say about it is that she's done with men. I'm afraid you've got your work cut out for you."

Nick wasn't sure why Julia had kept the details about Bernard the scam artist from her good friend but had entrusted them to him. Whatever the reason, it gave him an odd sense of accomplishment.

"I'm not interested in her that way." That got him Lainie's give-me-a-break look, and he grinned. "Okay, maybe a little. Mostly because we're nothing alike, so we have a lot to talk about. But it's not going to turn into anything other than friendship."

"Uh-huh. You just keep telling yourself that."

Any other time, he'd have come up with a witty comeback and strolled away. But for the second time that evening, a woman left him staring after her, completely at a loss for words.

Pushing the awkward conversation from his mind, he went inside and paused behind a back pew to look around. Like the rest of the town, the chapel was a simple frame building that hadn't changed much in its long history. Small but immaculately maintained, its claim to fame were six tall stained-glass windows that depicted scenes from the Bible. Even now, it amazed him that something so fragile had managed to survive nor'easters and blizzards since the early 1800s.

A couple of the moms spotted him, and their glares reminded him that a lot of folks in town still regarded him as the pastor's son gone wrong. Since he'd made only quick visits—and very few of those—in the years since his wild teenage days, he'd escaped the worst of the disapproving stares and whispered comments. Fortunately, his skin was even thicker now than it had been a few years ago, and he couldn't care less what they were gossiping about. He waved in their direction, amused when they flounced their shoulders and pointedly turned away. Not exactly subtle, he thought with a grin, but no different than they'd been in high school.

In a back corner, he noticed an old buddy hunched over a toolbox and sauntered over to say hello. Offering his hand, he said, "Hey, Ben. How've you been?"

All-county in every sport but badminton, Ben Thomas had the outdoorsy look of someone who spent a lot more time outside than Nick did. His wide-open face lit up in the kind of smile you didn't see very often, and he stood to shake Nick's hand. "Doing great. How 'bout you?"

Nick bit back his usual sarcasm and replied, "Just fine. Last I heard, you were working construction with your dad."

"Still am. Folks around here are always looking to build something. Lainie told me you started your own magazine on the internet. How're you liking that?"

"It's a lot of work, but most days I enjoy it."

A booming, all-too-familiar voice called out Ben's name, and Nick's blood froze in his veins. How could he have been so stupid? Of course the pastor would be here, overseeing the Christmas pageant.

In a single heartbeat, Nick was twelve again, planted in the front pew between Lainie and his mother, listening to another sermon about how God welcomed the righteous into heaven and condemned the wicked to eternal suffering. Even then, he'd known that a boy responsible for his brother's death was as wicked as they came.

Nick sensed someone watching him, and for some reason his eyes went straight to Julia. She locked gazes with him, smiling encouragement just before his father stormed into the chapel and stopped dead in his tracks. Out of sheer, stubborn pride, Nick forced himself to meet the pastor's eyes directly. "Hi, Dad."

"What are you doing here?"

The harsh greeting felt like a slap, and for the

life of him, Nick couldn't come up with anything other than a steely glare.

"He's helping me, sir," Ben replied quickly. "I needed an extra set of hands."

Nick hadn't done a thing even remotely helpful, but he appreciated Ben standing up for him. As his anger cooled into the boiling range, he answered for himself. "Julia invited me to come along, and I thought it'd be fun to watch Hannah."

Nick caught something in his father's eyes he'd never seen before: a glimmer of respect. He congratulated himself for coming up with the only answer that would prevent a very public display of McHenry temper.

"Your mother will be happy to see you." His flat tone made it clear his own feelings ran in the other direction. "Ben, I wanted to discuss a few things about the manger set with you."

With that, he turned on his heel and hurried away. Ben flashed Nick an apologetic smile and followed after him, scribbling notes while the pastor dictated what he had in mind. Once they were gone, Nick found a shadowy spot in a back pew and gratefully sank into it.

He'd come back to his father's church and survived an encounter with the dictator himself. Maybe there was something to this Christmas-spirit thing after all. From the entryway, he heard a gasp and turned to find his mother staring at him, mouth open in a huge smile.

As she rushed toward him, he smiled back and stood up. "Hi, Mom."

"Nick, I'm— I don't know the word. It's so wonderful to have you here again."

"Thanks."

After a warm hug, she beamed proudly up at him. "How are you and Julia doing?"

The way she said it, he got the impression she was reading more into his decision to stay in town than she should. "We're just working together, but it's going fine."

She gave him a long mother's look that said she doubted she was getting the whole story, but she let the comment go. "Have you decided how long you're staying?"

"Through Christmas." He grinned. "Or 'til Hannah gets sick of beating me at Chutes and Ladders, whichever comes first."

"I'm so glad you're spending some time with the kids. We just love them to pieces." Pausing, she lowered her voice to a motherly whisper. "It can't be easy coming back to the chapel after so many years. God bless you for putting that all behind you."

Her blessing raised the hackles on his neck, and he fought to keep his response quiet. "I'm sorry to disappoint you, but nothing's changed."

Regret flashed across her face, but as usual, she recovered quickly. "Well, I don't care why you're here. I'm just glad to see you." He was more than a little shocked to hear a cell phone ringing in the pocket of her sweater. She checked the caller ID and sighed. "Oh, this can't be good. Hello, Phyllis."

Nick moved to go, but she snagged his elbow to keep him from leaving. "I'm sorry to hear that, honey. Don't you worry a bit, just concentrate on getting rid of that pneumonia. I'll add you to the prayer list, and we'll hope to see you soon."

When she switched off her phone, she focused back on him with a thoughtful look that made him want to squirm. "What?"

"Do you still play the piano?"

Raising his hands in self-defense, he took a healthy step back. "Not since you finally let me quit taking lessons from you fifteen years ago."

"You were very good," she goaded, adding a flattering smile. "I wouldn't be a bit surprised to find you still remember most of what you learned."

"If you need an accompanist tonight, why don't you do it?"

"I can't play down here—" she motioned to the upright piano that sat to the left of the raised stage "—and be up there conducting the choir."

"What about Lainie?"

"She's downstairs making costumes." Tilting her head, she pegged him with an exasperated look. "Can you sew?"

She knew the answer to that question, and he cast about for another solution. After a quick assessment of the singers, he came up with something logical. "They're Christmas hymns, Mom. Everyone must know them well enough to sing *a cappella* this one time."

"In case you haven't noticed, half the choir is under the age of twelve, and some of the adults can't carry a tune in a bushel basket. If you could give them the melody line to follow, it'd be a big help."

Nick hated to let her down, but it had become a habit, and he firmly held his ground. If he wasn't careful, she'd have him playing Joseph before the evening was done. Folding his arms, he shook his head. "I'm just here to observe."

The joy shining in her eyes when she first saw him dimmed, and she nodded stiffly. "I'm sure we'll manage."

She turned to go up front, and Nick felt like an absolute heel. She had no idea how Christmas hymns grated on his nerves, and he couldn't bring himself to tell her. Generous to a fault, Ann McHenry had devoted her life to being the pastor's wife, mothering his church flock as if they were her own children. Cheerful and giving, everyone in town adored her.

Including her son, Nick thought with a frown. Even when he messed up, she loved him. Over the years he'd been away, her letters had kept coming, giving way to emails with family pictures attached. He seldom replied, but no matter where he was living at the time, she never let him stray too far away. Whenever he saw her name in his lengthy email list, he opened her message first. It was because of her that he'd traveled here for Thanksgiving—this year, for the first time, she'd begged him.

Time goes by so fast, Nick, she'd written. *Please answer my prayers and come home, just for a few days.*

Terrified that someone was sick, he'd immediately called Lainie and been relieved to hear everyone was healthy. But his talk with Julia a couple of days ago was a painful reminder that his family was ailing in a different way. Hearing about how she'd picked up the pieces of her life and moved on made him wonder if his family could somehow do the same. The problem was they'd been disjointed for so long, he wasn't sure he could do anything about it now.

Then again, he reminded himself, nothing ventured nothing gained.

He'd adopted that as his motto when he'd

taken an enormous personal and financial leap and founded *Kaleidoscope*. After several nerve-wracking bumps along the way, it was gradually becoming what he wanted it to be. Maybe returning to his father's church and helping out with the pageant rehearsal would turn into the beginning of something more. At least he could try.

Waiting until Mom was up on stage talking to the chorus, Nick strolled down the side aisle to the piano. A music book was propped on the stand, with a list of songs next to it. The first one was "O Holy Night." Though it was far from his own taste, he recalled it being one of his mother's favorites. Maybe if he concentrated on the piano part and ignored the words, he could get through it.

Sitting on the bench, he skimmed the music and decided he could probably handle the mellow song without butchering it too badly. His music lessons had ended ages ago, but he managed to find middle C and arched his hands into the position he'd learned as a child. The chords weren't difficult, and he'd just leave out any notes he didn't recognize. When he began softly playing, his mother whirled around to look down at him.

The delighted expression on her face was all the reward he needed, and he grinned up at her. "Does that key work for your choir, Mrs. McHenry?"

"Absolutely. Thank you."

A deeper, more personal emotion twinkled in her eyes, and he winked back in reply. Her bright laughter rang through the front of the chapel, and people looked around to find the reason for it. When they noticed him at the piano, heads leaned together and a predictable murmur rippled through the chapel.

From nowhere, Hannah popped up beside him. "Can I sit with you, Uncle Nick?"

She was so cute, he couldn't help grinning at her. "Don't they need the head angel?"

"Mommy's doing my costume, and I know my lines." She folded her hands in a begging gesture. "Ple-e-e-ase can I stay here with you? I could turn the pages, like I do for Mommy when she plays."

Offered up with adoring blue eyes, the artless wheedling made him laugh, and he finally gave in. Just like he always did with her mother, he recalled with a big brother's sigh. These two sure did have his number. "Sure, munchkin. Come on up."

While she squirmed into place beside him, he felt as if someone was watching them, and he glanced up to discover it was Julia. After a moment, she gave him a slow smile, her eyes sparkling with appreciation. Aside from his mother, he couldn't recall ever seeking a woman's approval. Julia's settled nicely into a corner of his heart he'd never thought much about. Until now.

Sitting at a beat-up old piano with a bubbly little girl chattering beside him, plunking his way through dusty old Christmas hymns, Nick got the sinking feeling he was in danger of losing his bad-boy status.

The strange thing was, he didn't really mind all that much. That was the moment when he knew for sure he was in trouble. And it was all Julia Stanton's fault.

"You've been holding out on me," Julia accused Nick while they strolled back to her shop. "I had no idea you were a musician."

"I wouldn't go that far," he replied with a wry grin. "Mom insisted on teaching us the piano when we were kids, and we all sang in the choir. She said we were Irish and music was in our blood, so we had an obligation to keep up the family tradition." After a few moments, he quietly added, "Of the three of us, Ian was the most talented. He had a great voice and a real knack for picking up different instruments."

During the week, Nick had made a few stray comments like that about his brother, completely out of the blue. Julia assumed their painfully honest conversation about Ian had cracked open the door into his past, and he was reluctant to fully close it again. Hoping to draw him out even further, she asked, "Do you discuss Ian with many people?"

"Never." Grimacing, he jammed his hands into his coat pockets. "I'm not even sure why I keep bringing him up with you. I guess you're just easy to talk to."

"I'm glad to hear that." Pausing on the sidewalk in front of Toyland, she pulled him to a stop. When she had his full attention, she added, "We all need someone to talk to once in a while. You can tell me anything, and I promise to keep it to myself."

As a grin slowly spread across his face, the twinkling lights in the window reflected back at her from his eyes. "I know," he said quietly. "That's weird because I don't trust very many people. But you're—"

"Different?" she suggested as the cool breeze plucked at her hair.

"Special." Reaching out, he tucked the stray wisp of hair back under her hat. With a thoughtful smile, he traced the curve of her cheek with his finger. "But you must hear that all the time."

Mesmerized by the admiration glowing in his eyes, she couldn't come up with a coherent response. All she could manage to do was shake her head. His chiseled features took on a warmth she hadn't seen before, and he leaned in as if he meant to kiss her.

Abruptly, he pulled away and took a healthy step backward. Julia couldn't decide if she was relieved or disappointed.

"I should get back before Lainie sends out a search party for me."

Wanting to keep him there just a little longer, she asked, "How's my story coming along?"

"The next installment runs on Sunday, so you can judge for yourself."

"I'm still not sure I want to," she confessed with a laugh. "The intro was very good, but that was just background about my parents and me. Did you put a nice spin on my childhood?"

"Yeah." He acted like he wanted to say something more, but he clamped his mouth shut firmly. "Good night."

After he got settled in his car, he cast a long look out the passenger window at her. She was no mind reader, but it appeared to her that he was acting like a man who didn't want to leave. Ignoring the alarms going off in her head, she tapped on the window and waited for him to lower it. "Would you like to come in for some hot cocoa?"

Flashing her that wicked grin, he warned, "If I come up to your apartment this time of night, the biddies'll never let you hear the end of it."

"People talk about me all the time as it is. How much worse could it get?"

"If you don't walk away right now, you'll find out."

All her life, Julia had done the proper thing, and look where it had gotten her. It was long past time she stopped caring about what people thought and did what she wanted.

So she crossed her arms in a determined pose and stood her ground. Laughing, Nick rolled up the window and rejoined her in front of the door. "You're sure about this?"

"Oh, for goodness' sake," she chided while she unlocked the door and let him in. "We're just having hot cocoa."

He flashed her a crooked grin. "Good cover. I'll back you up."

"I don't—"

He silenced her with a kiss so startling, it made her gasp. Though she'd almost hoped for something like this earlier, the reality of it made her head spin. Framing her face in his hands, he gazed at her with something she couldn't begin to define. "I've been wanting to do that all night."

Once she found her voice, she managed to stammer, "You did it very well."

Mischief lit his eyes, and he was about to say something when a sharp rapping on the front door made her jump. Framed in the glass was Daniel McHenry, looking like a furious thundercloud. Pointing at Nick, he motioned for his son to join him out on the sidewalk.

"Busted," Nick joked, but even in the dim light Julia could see he was trying to control his own temper. While part of her was relieved by the interruption, she still wished it was anyone else at the door. The brief encounters she'd observed between father and son snapped with tension, as if both were barely restraining the urge to strangle the other.

"This is silly," she announced, moving toward the door. "You don't have to talk out on the street when there's plenty of room in here. I'll invite him in for a snack, and I'll leave you two alone so you can talk like normal people."

Nick appeared on the verge of refusing, and she tilted her head, willing him to agree. She hadn't known him long, but one thing she'd learned quickly: he was as stubborn as they came. Unfortunately for him, her international experience had made her adept at convincing people to consider other possibilities. It was a skill she'd picked up from her father, and she decided to use it now.

"Just hear him out," she suggested in her most reasonable tone. "If you don't like what he has to say, you can leave."

"Promise?"

It was impossible to resist the playful glimmer in his eyes. She hadn't noticed it before, and it was a pleasant surprise to find there was still a little boy inside the hard-driving editor. "Promise. May I let him in now?"

"Whatever," he muttered with a shrug. "It's your shop."

Far from careless, she recognized the response as something he did when he wasn't thrilled with something but couldn't see a way around or out of it. It seemed to be his way of putting some distance between a tough situation and a surprisingly tender heart.

The revelation startled her, but she put it out of her mind and opened the door for her latest guest. "It's pretty cold out there, so I was about to make some cocoa. Would you like to come in and have some?"

The pastor frowned, as if he hadn't considered the possibility of being invited inside. "Thank you, Julia, but no. I want to talk to you," he added, glowering at Nick.

"That's a switch," Nick retorted. "You've been avoiding me for the past week."

"This isn't the place for us to discuss family business."

Glancing around, Nick met his father's glare with a calmness that alarmed her. "It's as good a place as any."

Julia's instinct was to leave them alone, but she couldn't retreat without drawing attention to herself. Instead, she stood quietly, praying they'd be able to reach some kind of truce before she was forced to intervene.

"Fine," Daniel relented. "I want to talk to you about accompanying the choir for the Christmas pageant."

"And you don't want Mom to hear what you have to say. That must mean you know it'd make her mad."

"It would, and I'd prefer to avoid that."

"What do you want, Dad?" The way Nick crossed his arms told Julia he knew precisely what the pastor was about to say, and he wasn't happy about it.

"You've allowed your relationship with God to dwindle away to nothing. That's your choice, but as the pastor of the church, it's my duty to make sure everyone connected with our Christmas service appreciates the significance of what we're celebrating."

"So because I don't worship, I can't play the piano?"

Daniel looked taken aback to hear it stated so bluntly, but he quickly recovered. "I wouldn't have put it quite that way, but yes, that's the gist."

Even to Julia's ears, the excuse sounded weak. "Daniel, that's not fair. We were in a real jam tonight, and without Nick's help the rehearsal would've been a disaster."

As his look passed from his son to her, it softened considerably. "Ann and I are very fond of you, and I honestly appreciate you trying to smooth things over. But this is between Nick and me."

"Phyllis has pneumonia," Nick pointed out. "She'll probably be in bed for a couple weeks."

Daniel folded his hands in front of him in a determined pose. "We'll find someone else."

"Anyone but me, right, Dad?"

They stared at each other for several tense moments, each sizing up the other. Julia could only imagine what was going through their minds, but if this was how all their encounters ran, it was easy to see why they'd drifted so far apart. The chasm between them was filled with icy bitterness, accumulated over years of practice. Right now, it looked uncrossable.

Daniel looked as if he wanted to say something, but then he shook his head and turned to go. He hadn't gone more than a few steps before he stopped abruptly. Clutching his chest, he reached for the back of a chair to steady himself.

Before she could blink, Nick was beside his father, a strong arm wrapped around his back. As he supported Daniel, he murmured, "Take it easy, now. The EMTs are right down the block at the firehouse. Julia, get them over here and then call Lainie and Mom."

"No, no," the older man insisted in a faint voice. "Don't worry them over nothing. I'm fine."

Ignoring his feeble protests, Nick helped him to the sofa and turned up the gas flames. Cell phone in hand, Julia made her calls as she raced upstairs for some pillows and a quilt to cover the shivering pastor. Once he was as comfortable as possible, Nick pulled up a wing chair and kept a watchful eye on him. Out of things to do until the paramedics arrived, Julia did the only thing she could.

Sitting on the arm of Nick's chair, she took his hand and gave it an encouraging squeeze. To her amazement, he didn't pull away. Instead, he wove his fingers through hers and gave her a grateful look. "Thanks."

"You're welcome."

Nick had never seen his father this way.

Lying on the white hospital sheets, he looked even paler than he had at Toyland. A tangle of cords monitored his vital signs, and Nick occupied himself by counting the beeps of the machine keeping track of his heart. Each one meant he was still alive, and Nick was thankful for each one.

Despite their torturous relationship, he loved his father deeply—and in this case, he loved him enough to respect what he was sure would be his father's wishes. Nick remained in the doorway, watching from a distance like a curious stranger. While his mother and Lainie fussed and scolded, he felt very much out of place, as if he belonged anywhere but here.

Julia appeared beside him with two cups of vending-machine coffee and handed one to him. "He's going to be fine, you know. You should go in and talk to him."

Shaking his head, Nick blew on his coffee to cool it down. After a sip, he added, "Fighting with me is what put him here in the first place. I don't want to make things worse."

"Is that what you think? That you gave him a heart attack?"

"That's what happened."

"He has angina," she corrected him in a hushed voice. "Lainie told me he's had it for a couple of years now, and every once in a while it flares up. Each time, the doctor runs tests, declares him fit to leave and sends him home with orders to take his medicine and slow down a little. For a while he does, then it's back to his old ways."

"Stubborn."

"I'd say it runs in the family." She met Nick's sharp look with the sweetest smile he'd ever seen. "Oh, come on. You know it's true."

Because it was pointless to debate something

so obvious, he chuckled. "Yeah, I guess. When you're double-Irish, there are plenty of hard heads to go around."

"Some people consider that a virtue. I happen to be one of them."

Despite the roller-coaster evening he'd had, Nick felt himself smiling at her. "Good to know."

He appreciated her standing in the hallway with him this way. It made him feel slightly less like an outcast, and his taut nerves gradually began to relax. When Lainie approached them, he braced himself. "Everything okay?"

"He's fine." She echoed Julia with the same brand of sympathy in her eyes. Only he knew it was different for Lainie because she understood how he was feeling. "Do you want to come in?"

Nick was stunned to discover that he did, very much. But he hesitated, anxious about upsetting Dad any more than he already had. "You think it's okay? I mean, I don't want to stress him out."

"You won't, and I think it'll do you good. You can try to hide it behind that tough-guy facade, but you still look like a semi ran you down."

He glanced to Julia, who politely kept her opinion to herself. But he saw the concern shadowing her eyes, and he heaved a resigned sigh. "All right, I'll admit I was terrified. Happy now?"

Laughing quietly, Lainie kissed his cheek.

"Why don't you both come in and say hi? He'll be glad to see you."

Julia greeted the pastor easily, leaning in for a quick hug before gracing him with one of her beautiful smiles. "How are you feeling?"

"Old and rickety," he grumbled, glancing up at Nick. "Thank you for catching me, son."

It was the first time in years that he could recall his father referring to him that way, and in spite of all the turbulence between them, he felt gratitude welling in his chest. He wanted to reach out a hand, the way Julia did so easily with people but dismissed the impulse and simply grinned. "No problem."

From her chair on the other side of his bed, Mom cleared her throat and nudged Dad with one of her looks. They stayed locked in one of their silent battles for several moments before he relented with a nod. Looking up at Nick, he said, "I want to apologize for the way I behaved earlier. The pageant is your mother's project, and I had no right to interfere with her choice of accompanist."

When he stopped speaking, she prodded, "And?"

He cut her a frustrated glance before focusing on Nick again. "If you'd like to fill in, we'd very much appreciate your help. Both of us," he added, earning a nod of approval from his wife.

Extracted from a man who'd just narrowly

escaped a heart attack, it wasn't the kind of whole-hearted gesture he'd been hoping for. But that his father had made it at all was so astounding, Nick decided to put aside his disappointment and take what he could get.

"Sure, Dad. I'd be glad to. It'll be fun getting to know Hannah's friends."

From the cloud that descended over Dad's expression, he knew that wasn't the kind of Christmas spirit-filled response the pastor had been anticipating. Unfortunately, it was the best Nick could do.

Chapter Six

After dropping their parents at the rectory, Nick and Lainie headed for her place. It was past midnight, and as a night owl, he was just getting warmed up. "Why didn't I know Dad had angina?"

"He hates thinking about it, so we don't mention it. He hasn't had an episode in over a year, so Mom and I assumed he was better."

"'Til I came home and just about gave him a heart attack."

She didn't contradict him, which only made him feel worse. "What were you two fighting about anyway?"

Nick filled her in on their argument, and she reached over to hug his arm. "For what it's worth, us Martin girls loved having you there tonight. Hannah said she thought it was awesome."

"Thanks."

They drove a mile in silence, and then she nudged his shoulder. "I held dinner for you, you know. Did you get lost on your way home?"

"No, brat, I walked Julia home after rehearsal and we got to talking."

"That's not what I heard. Georgia Bynes from the bakery was out walking her dog and saw you two in Julia's shop—not talking."

Perfect, he groaned inwardly. How was he going to explain that? Inspiration struck, and he joked, "There may have been mistletoe involved."

She clucked in disbelief. "There's not a single twig of mistletoe in that store."

In all honesty, Nick wouldn't recognize the plant if it sprouted to life in front of him. Since she had him dead to rights, he decided the best course was to let it go. "Don't read anything into it. We're just friends."

"Friends with mistletoe." She giggled. "Sounds like the title of a romantic Christmas movie."

Now that she'd brought it up, he replayed his intimate moment with Julia in his mind. It was moronic and totally unlike him to dwell on something that he'd already decided could never happen again, but he couldn't help it. Even though he'd surprised her, Julia's instinctive reaction had been warm and inviting, telling him he wasn't the only one feeling whatever it was he was feeling.

Frowning, he had to admit he didn't really understand what was happening to him. He was a planner, relying on a solid life strategy to keep him on track. That strategy included companionship strictly for fun. That way, the lady in question wouldn't be upset when things had run their course and it was time for him to move on.

Tonight, though, he couldn't make himself walk away. He'd tried to put some distance between them, but Julia had reached across the gap and pulled him back in. Considering the disastrous way her last relationship had ended, he couldn't believe she trusted him enough to let him so close. She was the first woman he'd met who'd asked him to stay when he was on his way out. Then again, she was the first one to offer him hot cocoa, too.

No matter what angle he viewed it from, their quick friendship baffled him. It just wasn't like him, and that made him antsy. He was always in control, but couldn't shake the sensation that he was falling into something he couldn't begin to understand. The idea that he'd lose his self-control with a sentimental woman who owned a toy store in a town on the edge of civilization was absurd.

But he couldn't deny that she fascinated him. Why, he couldn't say, but there it was all the same.

When they got back to the house, Todd met Lainie at the door with a warm hug. "I'm glad your dad's okay. How's Ann doing?"

"Relieved. Annoyed. When we left their place, she'd crammed his medicine down his throat and was trying to get him to lie down. How were the kids for you?"

"Baths and bed, no problem. I didn't want Hannah to worry, so I just told her you were with your parents."

"That works." Smiling, she looked at the papers stacked on the kitchen table. "How are your students' history reports?"

"A mixed bag, but you expect that this time of year," he replied as he filled his mug with some kind of tea and sat down. "Daydreaming about Christmas is way more fun than writing five pages about the Industrial Revolution."

"Speaking of writing," Nick said, "I should get to work on Julia's article. We're running the next installment on Sunday."

"Writing now?" Lainie asked with a yawn. "Are you serious?"

"Layouts and editing have to be done during the day, when other people are working. I write better at night anyway. It's quiet, and I don't get interrupted."

She gave him an understanding look. "You're having fun writing again, aren't you?"

"It's been a while since I ran with my own story, but it's going well so far." He chuckled. "I think."

After saying goodnight to them, he strode through the living room on his way upstairs. Todd had a fire going, and along with the lights on the Christmas tree, it was a nice, cozy scene. For some reason, his eyes were drawn to the large picture hanging on the wall above the fireplace.

A posed family shot from their wedding, it was in a gilded frame that clearly said it was important to Lainie and Todd. In spite of the smiles, it was a chilly arrangement, with Nick and his father standing on opposite sides as far from one another as they could get. On the mantel beneath it was a collection of Martin and McHenry family photos. One in particular caught his eye, and he lifted it from its spot.

It was a candid shot of Ian, Lainie and him, lined up front to back by height. There was a canoe beside them and tents in the background. Church camp, he recalled with a frown. A month before Ian died.

He heard someone come up behind him and felt Lainie's hand on his arm. "That's one of my favorites."

"That's nice." As he put the picture back in place, he was surprised to hear himself add, "Y'know, I really wish things were different."

Lainie put an arm around his shoulders, the way he'd seen her do with Hannah when she was upset. "What things?"

"That." Nick nodded at the incomplete wedding family photo. "Ian should've been there with us."

"He was." When he looked over, she gave him a gentle smile. "Whenever we're all together, I feel him there, too."

"How?"

"As long as we love someone, they're never really gone."

He recognized that she'd skirted around the religion issue but still managed to get her point across. "Wish I could believe that."

"So do I."

Kissing his cheek, she patted his shoulder in a comforting gesture before heading upstairs. After she left, he stood there for a long time, staring at that picture, longing for something that could never be.

Saturday at Toyland was like a zoo, and Julia was grateful for the distraction.

All those customers kept her from thinking about Nick. Well, mostly. Whenever she didn't have much to do, the memory of their brief encounter slipped into her thoughts. More than once, she'd run it through her mind, curious about what had come over her. Was it a mistake? she asked herself for the hundredth time.

The memory of that tender moment still made her smile, and she had to admit that crazy as it seemed, she considered it anything but a mistake. Wise? No. Wonderful? Definitely. She wasn't some brainless twit who swooned when a man kissed her, but with Nick she'd felt something unique. What, she couldn't say exactly, but it had been there that night, and it hadn't faded.

But how did Nick feel about it? She hadn't heard from him since their race to the hospital, and she couldn't help wondering if his disappearing act was some kind of message. Maybe he regretted kissing her, assuming she'd expect more of the same if he came around again.

Maybe he was right to keep his distance. Because she had no intention of getting serious with anyone right now, she'd resolved to keep a solid grip on her emotions. Her mission was to reconcile Nick and his father—not fall in love with the prickly editor.

Fall in love? Where on earth did that idea come from?

"Excuse me."

Fortunately, a customer pulled her back to more practical matters. She firmly pushed thoughts of Nick aside and plastered a smile on her face. "May I help you?"

"You've got different gauge train sets, and I'm not sure which one is best for our son," the man explained.

"How old is he?"

"Two."

Muting a laugh, she explained, "Those have a lot of tiny parts, so they're meant for older kids and adults. What you want is back here."

She led him to another display she'd set up just like the ones in front. The only difference was that the train winding beneath the tree was a sturdy wooden set, ideal for small fingers.

"Perfect," he agreed with a relieved smile. "I'll take two."

"Two?"

"One for us, one for your Gifting Tree. It's a great idea, and I'll feel good knowing some little kid will have a nice Christmas."

"That's very generous," she approved as she carried the two boxes up to the counter. "Thank you."

"Are you getting a lot of help with it?" he asked while he signed the charge slip.

Not as much as she'd hoped for, but she didn't want to complain to him when he'd just purchased a fairly expensive gift for a stranger. "People do what they can."

"Do you have any flyers?" When she shook her head, he said, "I work at a PR firm over in Oak-bridge. I can pass the word around there if you want. That should help."

Wary of creating the impression that she was seeking recognition for what should be open-hearted charity, she'd never considered advertising her toy drive. Then the full meaning of what he'd said hit her, and the light bulb went off. Offering her hand across the counter, she said, "Julia Stanton. How would you like to earn a little extra money during the holidays?"

"Aaron Coleman. What did you have in mind?"

"Helping me spread the word about my Gifting Tree. With some expert help, I imagine I could double the response I'm getting on my own. What do you say?"

Grinning, he reached into his wallet and took out a business card. "I say give me a call on Monday. I'll have some ideas for you by then."

"And a simple contract for me to sign?"

Another grin. "Actually, I'd trade the PR work for the trains."

"Done." Opening the order screen, she voided the transaction and credited his account. "Merry Christmas."

"To you, too." Grabbing the handle on the box holding his son's present, he waved with his free hand. "Talk to you Monday."

As Julia watched him go, she couldn't keep back a smile. You never knew when God would send you just what you needed, sometimes even when you didn't realize you were missing anything in the first place. You just had to keep your eyes—and your mind—open to the possibilities.

Once more, Nick snuck into her thoughts. Her inability to keep him at bay made her wonder if there might be possibilities with him, too.

Saturday afternoon, Nick was finishing up his draft. When he first started *Kaleidoscope,* he did everything himself, from writing to final layout. These days, he oversaw all aspects of the business, but he hadn't produced any significant content of his own in almost two years. It was humbling to remember just how much went into the writing process. He almost felt sorry for the reporters he dogged on a regular basis.

Then again, it would do them good to see the boss with his own byline. It would prove he knew what he was talking about when he hacked up their work before approving it for *Kaleidoscope'*s growing readership.

When he was done with the rough draft of his text, he flipped through the stack of childhood photos Julia had loaned him for scanning. He narrowed them down to two, one of which would accompany the latest article. The first was of her and her mother with their violins. In the willowy Gisele Stanton, with her graceful pose and encouraging smile, he saw how Julia would look in twenty years or so.

The other was of Julia swathed in pink netting, dressed for her role in *The Nutcracker.* She looked to be around seven or eight, with her hair braided and piled on top of her head. Eyes bright with excitement, she stood in a graceful ballet pose, smiling at the photographer.

Since everyone kept reminding him it was Christmastime, he went with the ballet pic. It complemented the story on her unusual childhood perfectly. He set up Todd's ancient scanner, sitting back while it slowly processed the photo. Only one problem, he thought while he waited.

To finish the exposé, he needed more interviews with Julia. Considering the way things had gone the last time they were together, he was torn between wanting to see her and avoiding her completely. As the scanned photo gradually unfolded onto his monitor, he rolled the two options over in his mind, weighing the pros and cons of each.

When the picture scan was complete, so was his analysis. Dead-even, he realized with a sigh. What was he supposed to do with that?

"Do you always sigh at your computer?"

Nick twisted around to find Lainie in the doorway holding an armload of winter clothes. "Sometimes. Did you need something?"

"We're going sledding. You'll freeze in those fancy duds you packed, so I brought you some of Todd's things to wear."

"Thanks, but I've got a lot to do."

Walking up behind him, she leaned in to read

over his shoulder. "The layout box is full, so you must be done."

"The draft is finished," he corrected her sharply. "It still needs a lot of tweaking, and then there's everything else in the edition that I need to approve."

"Oh, please! It's two o'clock, and we'll be back by four. You can tear yourself away for some fun and then tweak it after that." When he didn't say anything, she folded her arms with that mom look every kid hated. "Don't make me send Hannah up here."

"Y'know, I'm used to being the guy in charge," he reminded her, pointing to himself for emphasis. "I tell other people what to do, not the other way around."

"Maybe that's your problem," she shot back. "You steamroll people, so they never question you or push back with their own opinions, even if they have good ideas. You miss a lot that way."

Nick opened his mouth to let her have it, then realized she had a point about him missing things. In truth, she was echoing something that had begun dawning on him during the pageant rehearsal. For the first time in years, he was involved in Christmas, not just counting the days to his latest Caribbean holiday vacation. Much as he hated to admit it, he enjoyed seeing the decorations all over town and was even starting to get used to the endless stream of sappy music.

"Okay," he relented, shutting off his system before standing up. "Just a couple hours, though, and only because it's easier than arguing with you."

"You don't fool me for a second, big brother. You want everyone to think you're a cranky old bear, but deep down you're just a big softie."

"I'd appreciate you not spreading that around," he muttered. "It'd be bad for my image."

Laughing, she tossed her load of clothes on the bed and saluted him before executing a military turn and heading back into the hallway.

Picking through the pile, Nick chose two pairs of hunting socks, a heavy sweater and a grown-up version of the snow pants he'd worn when he was a kid. As he zipped himself into a parka with a warm hood, he flashed back to a time in his life when he'd dressed this way all the time, bundled against the bitter cold of a place he'd done everything in his power to forget. He remembered meeting Cooper, Ben and other buddies at Willow Pond, choosing up sides and playing hockey until dark.

Other days, they went straight home from school to grab their sleds and camping jugs full of warm water. Racing to a good-size hill out on the edge of town, they'd tramp down the newly fallen snow, watering it to make the track slicker.

That was where Lainie was taking her family now, and the realization made him stop in the middle of tying a knee-high snow boot. Desperate to escape his shameful past, he'd left behind all the memories Holiday Harbor represented to him. What he didn't understand until now was that in turning his back on the bad things, he'd lost sight of the good times, too.

Innocent and fun, they came back to him now in a flood of laughter he'd all but forgotten. And suddenly, the looming deadline for his magazine was the last thing on his mind. He couldn't wait to get back to Spinnaker Hill and see if—like the rest of the town—it really was the way he remembered it.

Julia couldn't believe her eyes.

When she arrived at the sledding hill, she immediately noticed Nick, clearly dressed in Todd's too-large outdoor clothes. He sat on an old log at the edge of things, cradling a quilted bundle that held his sleeping nephew.

"Watch me, Uncle Nick!" Hannah shouted, squealing when Todd gave their toboggan a shove and jumped on behind her and Lainie.

They made it about halfway down the long

track, and Nick laughed. "Your steering needs a little work, munchkin. Hey, Julia."

He was the most intense man she'd ever met, and seeing him so relaxed and at ease stunned Julia so much, at first she didn't know what to say. When she managed a feeble greeting, he gave her a puzzled look. "Something wrong?"

"Well, no," she stammered, which was very unlike her. She'd been schooled in every form of etiquette on the planet, and she was seldom at a loss for words. Laughing at herself, she shook her head. "I guess I didn't realize you had a laid-back side."

"It's been a while since I've let it show."

Noah shifted in his sleep, and the scarf covering his face slipped down a few inches. Nick pulled it up to leave just the boy's nose showing, and the smile he gave his sleeping nephew would have melted the iciest heart on the planet.

Unfortunately, Julia's was far from icy, and she couldn't keep back a smile of her own. Though he was the self-confessed black sheep of his family, she'd come to understand that Nick McHenry used his bad-boy status to conceal a generous heart. When you figured in his dark good looks, it could only add up to trouble for any girl trying to avoid romantic entanglements.

Yet for the first time since her trust had been shattered, Julia felt herself opening up to the idea of allowing another man into her life. This man. With his brooding manner and sharp wit, he appeared to be her opposite in every way. But seeing him with his niece and nephew, how gently he handled his mother and a difficult situation with his father, she'd begun piecing together a completely different picture of him. She wasn't sure she was ready to have feelings for a man again… but her foolish heart wasn't giving her much of a choice in the matter.

He brushed off a spot on the log for her. "Have a seat."

She hesitated, then realized she was being ridiculous. Standing her sled upright in the deep snow, she sat down beside him. She'd never had a problem coming up with something to talk about with him, but her old shyness chose that moment to resurface, and she searched for something to say.

Finally, she came up with a topic that seemed fairly safe. "How did you end up on babysitting duty?"

"Lainie and Todd kept taking turns going down with Hannah while the other hung on to Noah. I took a few runs, and then I offered to keep junior so she could have them both to herself for a while."

Spoken in a matter-of-fact tone, the simple answer impressed her far more than if he'd bragged about how great he was. "That's very thoughtful. I'm sure they really appreciate it."

"Give 'em a few more trips back up the hill," he said with a grin. "Then we'll see how they feel."

Sure enough, after about ten more minutes, Lainie trudged over and flopped down in the snow. "I know this hill wasn't this big when we were kids."

"Sure, it was," Nick teased. "You were just a lot younger back then."

When she stuck her tongue out at him, Julia knew she'd gotten a glimpse of how the two of them had acted when they were growing up. Lighthearted and happy, the way they would have been before Ian died. His death had altered the McHenrys in so many ways, some large, some small. Some changes had been unavoidable, but others had mushroomed simply because no one knew how to stop them. She renewed her promise to do everything in her power to break down those barriers and bring happiness back to this family that had been so kind to her.

"I'll take Noah." Lainie held her arms out. "You and Julia should get to have some fun, too."

Seeming to sense her uneasiness, Nick cocked his head at Julia with a questioning look. "Is that okay with you?"

Shaking off her shyness, she nodded her head. "Sure." Grinning, she added, "But I get to steer."

"Why am I not surprised?" The gleam in his eyes took the sting out of his grumbling, and they strolled across the wide hilltop to choose a clear starting spot.

Nick's gaze traveled a little farther out, where teenagers were doing tricks on snowboards and a few were grooming what looked to her like a narrow sheet of ice. "We used to do that," he said, nodding toward the daredevils. "Only back then, we just stood up on our sleds and went as far as we could. Ben was the craziest, so he usually won."

"Ben Thomas?" she asked. When he nodded, she laughed. "He's so responsible now, it's hard to imagine him risking his neck that way."

"Back then we thought nothing bad could ever happen to us."

She couldn't miss the subtle shift in his tone, from nostalgic to wistful. Talking about his past seemed to be getting easier for him, and she decided it was time to pry a little bit. "Before Ian died?"

"Yeah." Still focused on the boarders, he frowned. "That first winter, I didn't even come up here. Ben and Cooper kept asking, but I couldn't do it. Even after that, it was never the same without Ian."

Something in his response touched her, and she gently asked, "What was he like?"

"Better than me in every way you could imagine." Apparently finished with his walk down memory lane, he set her sled down and knelt in the back, digging his toes in to keep it in place. "Ready?"

"Nick, I'm sorry. I didn't mean—"

"Don't worry about it." The sorrow in his eyes eased a little, and he gave her one of those maddening bad-boy grins. "But if we keep yakking out here, folks are gonna think I came to chat with you instead of sled."

"Which would be bad for your image," she guessed as she settled into the front of the toboggan.

"Deadly. Ready?"

Grasping the steering rope firmly in her mittened hands, she nodded. "Ready."

Getting to his feet, he shoved off and gave them a running start before landing behind her with a thud. He reached around her and grabbed the handles to keep from falling off. After a few runs, they had a nice track and were getting a long ride. It wasn't even remotely romantic, but racing down that hill with Nick's arms around her was the most fun Julia had had in a very long time.

Inspired by the childish fun around her, she let herself fall backward into the snow and began waving her arms and legs.

Nick stared down at her with a look of disbelief. "Snow angels? Seriously?"

"Not serious at all," she assured him as she carefully stood to avoid ruining her impression. Admiring her handiwork, she asked, "What do you think?"

"Not bad," he said, chuckling as he shook his head. "I just wish I had a camera so folks would believe it."

"Everyone needs to have fun once in a while. Even you."

Without warning, she shoved with all her might, and he went down in a cloud of snow. Sitting up, he dangled an arm over his bent leg. "What was that for?"

"Fun."

"Not for me."

"Then for me," she retorted with a laugh. "I thought it was hilarious."

"Wonderful."

When he held out a hand in a silent request, she let out a very unladylike snort. "And let you pull me down? Not a chance."

Muttering under his breath, he picked himself up and fell in step beside her. While they were trudging up the hill, someone shouted, "Hey, McHenry!"

Looking up, she saw Cooper Landry standing at the top of the hill. Holding out two large, steaming containers, he grinned. "Wanna race?"

"Cooper." The name came out in a murmur, and Nick's normally stern features lit up with pure joy. In that moment, she glimpsed the boy he must have been and how much his childhood friend meant to him. It didn't last, though, and he bellowed back, "You sure your wife'll let you go?"

Bree poked her head out from behind Cooper. "Bring it on, smart-mouth."

Nick's laughter was unlike anything Julia had heard from him before. It was lighthearted and carefree, not the controlled, bitter-edged kind she was accustomed to. It struck her that during their first meeting, he'd been grumpy about Cooper's absence not because he was annoyed, but because he missed his old friend.

When they reached the top, Bree greeted her boss with a stern glare. "Okay, hotshot. Why didn't you come to the wedding?"

"Work." The smooth reply told Julia he used that excuse enough that it rolled easily off his tongue. "You know, that thing some of us do instead of shutting off our phones and sailing around the Caribbean for a month."

"Nice try," Cooper informed him, the mock-stern tone belied by his big grin and warm handshake. "We had a blast, and we're not a bit sorry."

Nick grinned back. "I'm glad, really. How'd you like the catamaran?"

"Awesome," Bree answered, trading a smile with her husband before adding, "It was really nice of you to arrange that for us."

Nick was about to say something when a black blur came barreling toward them. Stepping protectively between it and Julia, he held out both arms to stop a huge Newfoundland dog from running her down. Taking his cue, the dog slammed on the brakes and sat in front of Nick, his tail stirring up a whirl of snow.

"This must be the famous Sammy," Nick said, kneeling down to his level. Polite as always, the dog lifted his paw for Nick to shake. "It's great to meet the star of Bree's Holiday Harbor stories." To the humans gathered around, he added, "This ball of fur was a real hit with our readers. Lost dog rescued by local mayor—it was small-town Americana gold."

"That piece got my miserable career back on track." Ruffling his ears, Bree stepped back into Cooper's embrace. "Not to mention, if I hadn't come here, I'd never have met Cooper. All thanks to my new boss."

"Yeah, yeah, yeah," Nick grumbled, eyes twinkling in fun. "You're just pitching for a new assignment."

"As long as it's in northern Maine. With the

way the weather's been so far this winter, I'm not keen on traveling anywhere 'til spring."

"Enough shoptalk," Cooper announced, pointing toward his burgundy four-by-four parked nearby. "I've got extra water, and Ben's on his way with more. If we lay some down before he gets here, the track'll be ready quicker."

"We've only gone down a few times," Julia pointed out. "It's not packed down very much yet."

"We can fix that," Bree told her. "If we go together, we should be heavy enough to get a good track started."

With Bree in the front, Julia ran in and launched them along the broken snow. Their descent was quicker this time, and they ended up much farther down, laughing on their backs while they added more snow angels to the flock Julia had started. She'd spent her winters in wonderful places all around the world, skiing and skating, attending operas, ballets and formal balls. But nowhere had she enjoyed herself more than on this simple sledding hill overlooking the ocean.

Rolling over, she looked out toward the frozen harbor and saw the thing that had drawn her to this place on her first visit months ago.

Last Chance Lighthouse.

Built onto a rugged outcropping, it looked as if it had sprouted from the bedrock centuries ago.

Today, the old tower was nearly lost in a cloud of chilly fog and Julia asked, "How is Mavis doing in this weather?"

"She's fine. Cranky as ever. We stopped in to see her this morning, and she scolded us for staying away so long." Lying on her stomach, Bree tapped her boots together like a teenager sharing secrets with a friend. "Of course, she was feeding us gingerbread the whole time, so it wasn't as bad as it sounds."

"I worry about her out there all alone."

"Cooper made sure someone checked on her while we were gone. Now that we're back, she and I will be working on a history of Holiday Harbor, so I'll be spending a lot of time with her."

"Hey, this ain't a hen party!" Nick bellowed from the midpoint on the hill. "If all you're gonna do is gossip, then get outta the way."

"Whatever." After sending him a wilting look, Bree got to her feet and retrieved the sled. Offering Julia a hand, she murmured, "If we time it just right, we can run him over. Whattya say?"

It was completely unlike her to do such a thing, which of course made it that much more appealing. Giggling, Julia nodded and they ascended the hill arm in arm, trading news as they went. Near the top, she gave Bree a quick hug. "I know we haven't been friends very long, but I really missed you."

"I know what you mean. Some people just click, like we did. It's good to be home."

Home, Julia thought, looking around at the laughing groups of people enjoying the crisp afternoon. Old and young, brash and timid, all of them had other things to do, but they'd chosen to come here and spend the afternoon with each other.

This was the kind of feeling she'd been searching for her entire life. She loved knowing that she belonged somewhere and that someone other than her parents was kind enough to make her part of their family. That she'd found her place in this tiny fishing village on the coast of northern Maine was more than a surprise. It was a blessing.

Looking into the clear winter sky, she sent up a heartfelt prayer of gratitude. A warm feeling of contentment settled over her, letting her know God was listening.

Chapter Seven

Before Nick knew it, the sun was going down. Of course, this time of year that happened around five, but still, he hated to see the afternoon end. He hadn't had this much fun in years.

The ice track was a huge success, and the older kids were thrilled with it. When he overheard a couple of them making plans to pile up snow on the sides and build a half-pipe, he made a mental note to get a snowboard and try it out. Early some afternoon while the kids were all in school, just in case he stunk. The thought made him laugh.

"Something funny?" Cooper asked while they stacked empty water jugs back in his car.

"Just thinking. Where would I get a snowboard?"

"There's a new outdoor shop out on the highway between here and Sandy Cove. They've got all the latest stuff. I hear," he added quickly when Bree sent him a curious look.

Oblivious to the couple's exchange, Ben announced, "I'm starving. Anyone wanna hit The Albatross with me?"

Inside ten minutes, the nine of them were sitting around the largest table in the place, smack in the middle of the restaurant. Noah sat in his high chair, feeding pieces of cracker to Todd while Lainie patiently listened to Hannah read the words she knew from the menu out loud. Cooper and Ben were arguing about who'd had the best run, and Bree had her head together with Julia over something Nick was pretty sure he was better off not knowing about.

Sitting back, he soaked it all in with a smile. Normally, he was so busy that when he finally stopped working for the day all he wanted was some peace and quiet. Unfortunately, that meant his social life was almost nonexistent. He didn't have many friends away from the business that soaked up ninety percent of his waking hours. Once he got back to Richmond, he'd have to do something about that. When the most fun you'd had in three years was sledding in Maine, it was time to reassess.

When he noticed a waitress headed for their table, he bit back a groan. He'd forgotten that Lucy Wilson's parents owned the diner, and apparently she still helped out there. She looked less than pleased to see him, and he felt himself begin to stiffen reflexively, bracing for an unpleasant end to his happy afternoon. Then, out of nowhere, he heard himself say, "Hey, Lucy. How are you doing?"

Apparently, she suspected his friendly greeting was some kind of trick because her eyes narrowed. "Fine."

"Great." She didn't ask about him, but he pushed aside the annoyance and decided he'd done the best he could for now. "Before anyone else says otherwise, I'll take the check."

The men in the group protested but not very loudly. Julia smiled her approval, which was all the reward he needed. "That's very generous, Nick. Thank you."

"It's the least he can do," Ben mumbled through a mouthful of cornbread. "He hasn't paid since graduation night."

The entire table fell silent. Everyone there knew he hadn't been around to pick up tabs for meals, and some even knew what had kept him away for so long. Nick held his breath, waiting for someone to point out how selfish he'd been.

"We'll just have to punish him then," Julia announced, opening her menu to the seafood section. "I love their lobster bisque."

Laughing, everyone joked about ordering the most expensive items on the menu. Which, to be honest, would still make this the cheapest meal he'd bought for a group this size since he was in high school.

Beneath the table, he squeezed Julia's hand and leaned in to whisper his thanks.

Returning the gesture, she answered with an amazing smile that warmed him right down to his toes. If they weren't in public, he'd have been far too tempted to kiss her on the spot. When Lucy left after taking everyone's orders, he said to Julia, "I have a confession to make."

Stacking her elegant hands together, she rested her cheek on them and angled to face him. "Really? What's that?"

"I'm not done with the childhood section of your biography. The intro was no big deal, but this one's more complex, and I'd like your okay before I post it. I meant to have it to you by now, but my pest of a little sister hijacked me to go sledding."

Julia laughed, bringing to mind the jingle bells on the bracelet she had been wearing the first day he met her. "I'm so glad she did."

"Me, too." He smiled before going on. "But I still have to finish up. I was thinking, if I worked at your place, you could review the earlier part while I do the end. It'd save me some time if you don't mind doing it in pieces."

"That's fine with me, but don't you need your computer?"

Nick broke a breadstick and offered her half.

"I store everything online, so I can access it from anywhere."

"Very clever. Okay, we can head over together after we eat. Besides, I still owe you some hot cocoa. Mom just sent me a Swiss chocolate mix, and I haven't had a chance to try it yet. You can be my guinea pig."

"Gladly."

Before long, their food arrived, and everyone demolished their meal in record time. As the others said goodbye and got ready to leave, Nick went to the counter to settle up. He charged the food, but he wanted to do something nice for Lucy, to prove he wasn't the jerk she remembered from high school.

Reaching into his wallet, he took out two twenties and handed them to her. For lack of anything better, he said, "Merry Christmas."

"Right. You want change from this, I'm sure."

"No, it's yours. There were a bunch of us, and we were kinda rowdy. I appreciate you taking such good care of us."

"I… You… You're welcome," she stammered. And for the first time he could recall, she smiled at him. "Merry Christmas."

If that wasn't reward enough, when he glanced around for Julia, he found her standing near the door and wearing one of her gorgeous smiles.

As he approached, he made a show of looking around. "Is that smile for me?"

"Yes." He opened the door, and she glided through. "I think you made Lucy's day."

Ordinarily he'd have brushed it off, but this time he accepted the compliment. "In case you missed it, I don't have the best rep around town. I figured it's time to do something about that."

"Why now?" she asked as they strolled up the sidewalk.

He actually wasn't certain, but he came up with something reasonable. "It'll be better for the kids that way."

"So it doesn't matter to you what the people in town think of you, one way or the other?"

"Not really."

She didn't react to that, and he wondered if his attitude had upset her. That's what he got for being honest, he complained silently. To his surprise, she finally said, "Good for you. Bree's like that, too, and I wish I had a little of that confidence."

"Nah," he replied, pulling open the gilded door of Toyland. "Nice is more your style."

That made her laugh, and several heads turned when they walked in. She checked in with her two clerks, then told them, "Nick and I have some work to do upstairs. If you need anything, just come get me."

As they headed up, he admired her for announcing that so openly. Then again, if she blithely trotted up to her apartment with him in tow with no explanation at all, tongues would wag for hours. This way, anyone with nothing better to do would spread the news and move on to something more interesting.

Shakespeare was asleep on his perch, so there was no poetic greeting. More than a little disappointed, Nick took his coat off and hung it on the railing, then gestured downstairs with a tilt of his head. "I'm impressed. You're really getting the hang of living in this fishbowl."

"People talk about me even when I don't do anything," she explained in a resigned tone. "At least now they have a reason."

"Can't argue with that."

They both laughed, and she told him, "My laptop's in the spare room, so you can unplug it and bring it out here. I'll get started on the cocoa."

While she was gone, Nick retrieved the computer and set himself up on the sofa. By the time she brought their drinks in, he'd pulled up her bio and was skimming it for obvious problems. The rich scent of chocolate in his mug was outdone only by the creamy taste. "It's like melted candy."

"A good description." Taking a sip, she closed her eyes with a sigh. "There's nothing in the world like Swiss chocolate."

"My chocolate usually comes from the rack at the supermarket, so I'll have to take your word on that." Handing over the laptop, he warned, "I never let anyone read a piece at this stage, but I think you'll get the gist."

The section wasn't long, but the time he spent waiting for her to finish and give him an opinion felt like an eternity. Since he was at the top of the *Kaleidscope* food chain, Nick wasn't used to seeking approval from anyone on what he published. That humble feeling he'd experienced earlier crept in again, and he made a mental note to be nicer to his freelancers. Except for Bree. She irritated him on purpose, and he couldn't let her get away with that.

Fortunately, Julia was a quick reader. Looking over the screen, she smiled. "You're an excellent writer. You have a brisk, efficient style, but you focus on all the right details to give the reader a clear picture of your subject."

Her praise had a personal slant to it, and he couldn't help returning the smile. "It helps to have a good topic to start with."

Cradling her mug in her hands, she curled into a ball and angled to face him. "I know I've had an unusual life, and I appreciate you making my family seem as normal as possible. I hope that will continue when things get—"

She frowned, and he suggested, "Complicated?" When she nodded, he turned to look her directly in the eyes. "You've been through a lot, and I can't change that. But I can promise not to make it worse."

"Thank you."

The relief in her voice reminded him that she'd taken a huge risk in allowing someone she barely knew to write the story of her exceptional life. Nick wanted to make sure she never regretted her decision to trust him. "I'm gonna show them how you've moved on and made a great life for yourself, right here."

"You make it sound like your personal mission," she said gently. "Why do you care?"

"What that snake did to you..." Feeling his temper spike, he took a calming breath. "He took a lot more than your money. He humiliated you, and you pretty much went into hiding because of it. He stole this past year of your life from you, and you can't ever get that back."

"You sound angry."

"I'm furious," he corrected her with an intensity that almost frightened him. "Trust me, if I ever get a clue about where he is, that dirt bag will be under the nearest jail."

"I think you watch too many detective shows," she teased with a grateful smile. "But I appreciate the thought. It's very sweet, in a dangerous kind of way."

"Yeah, well, that's the kinda guy I am."

"I'm glad."

She added a warm hug that felt so incredible, he wished he could figure out a way to make it go on longer. That meant it was time to leave, so he drew back and rested his forehead on hers with a sigh. "I should go finish this article, but I really don't want to."

"Hmm…" Those amazing eyes glanced up at the ceiling, then settled back on him with a playful gleam. "I could invite you to stay a while longer. I need some help with the holiday goodies people keep bringing me. I'll never be able to eat them all myself before they get stale."

Forget caution, he decided. He couldn't turn down an invitation like that. "Yeah? What've you got?"

Laughing, she stood and headed for the kitchen. "Why don't you pick out a movie, and I'll put together a snack?"

Not that he needed a snack after the huge meal they'd eaten, but he'd have gone along with just about anything to avoid leaving. Whenever he was with her, he felt something that went way beyond happiness.

Contentment.

The two emotions were different, he realized as he surveyed the collection of holiday movies in the cabinet under the TV. More than fun, or joy, time with Julia left him with the firm belief that he was no longer missing something he wasn't even aware he'd wanted. Confusing but wonderful, he didn't have the words to accurately describe it.

Maybe, he thought as he pulled out a DVD case, that was what made it so special.

Julia appeared with a plate piled high with candies and cookies. "I pulled out a little of everything. What did you end up with?" Nick showed her, and her mouth fell open in astonishment. "*Miracle on 34th Street?* What made you pick that one?"

He'd chosen one of the longer ones she had, but he wasn't about to admit that to her. Instead, he shrugged. "I've never seen it. Is it okay with you?"

"More than okay," she assured him, setting the plate on the table before sitting back down. "It's my favorite."

"Oh, yeah?" Nick asked while he got the movie started. "Why's that?"

"The idea of having faith in something you can't prove, just because you know in your heart that it's real." Nibbling on a reindeer cookie, she added, "Plus, I like how the girl and her mom go from being cynical about love to believing in it."

Flinging himself onto the couch, he spread his

arms across the back and let out a groan. "Are you telling me this is a holiday chick flick? Perfect."

He'd thought he sounded pretty convincing, but she laughed. "You've got the grumbly bear act down pat. You must terrify the people who work for you."

"Everyone except Bree," he replied while he fast-forwarded through the previews. "I had no idea you two were such good friends. You're so different from each other."

"I know, but it works somehow. I like having a girlfriend to do things with."

I'd like that, too.

The thought came and went so quickly, he almost missed it. Before long, she was cuddled up beside him, and he found himself enjoying the sweet, sappy movie. As far from his usual Saturday night as he could possibly get, Nick caught himself wishing there was a way to make this evening go on forever.

Nick finally tore himself away from Julia's around eleven. She sent him back to Lainie's with a warm smile and a plate full of treats for the Martins. If they'd been in Richmond, he'd have invented a reason to dawdle, but this was Holiday Harbor. That kind of lingering would only cause trouble for Julia, and in spite of what she'd said earlier, he wasn't about to do anything to grease the wheels of the local gossip mill.

When he got back to Lainie's, the house was dark except for the light over the kitchen stove. A note on the table told him there was leftover meatloaf in the fridge if he wanted it, along with a squiggly-mouthed smiley face that told him his sister remembered just how much he hated meatloaf. After recycling the note, he stood in the living room with his hands in his back pockets. He had the strangest feeling he'd forgotten to do something, but he couldn't figure out what was missing from his very full day.

Deciding it would come to him eventually, he headed upstairs and got ready for bed. Lying there in the dark, every time he closed his eyes he saw Julia's face. Smiling, laughing, filled with gratitude for his handling of her very personal story. If he tried harder, he could hear her voice, with the soft lilt that he assumed was a blend of French and Midwestern, inherited from her parents.

They'd spent hours in interviews and just talking, and he'd come to love the sound of that voice. Gentle and sweet, with a hint of the steel he noted in her eyes when something was important to her. Somewhere along the line, when he wasn't paying attention, she'd become very special to him. And suddenly, he wanted to do something out of the ordinary for her. But what?

Selecting Christmas gifts wasn't his strength. Julia and Lainie had helped him buy things for the kids, and his ideas for the grown-ups in the family were practical. For Julia, he wanted something else. Something that would earn him one of those amazing smiles.

While he mulled various options, he searched his memory for a clue about what she might like. Then, clear as a bell, he recalled what she'd said when he'd been admiring the collection in her office.

Now that I'm settled, I'd love to get a dollhouse.

Rolling over, he grabbed his laptop from the bedside table and woke the screen. Typing in a search, he landed at a site in Modesto, California, that sold what he needed. Dollhouses. Not the little-kid kind, but miniature versions of mansions from across the world, large enough to hold Julia's impressive collection of furniture. The prices were extravagant, too, but the homes were custom-made and probably worth every penny. Clicking through the gallery, he landed on one called *The Vanderbilt* and grinned. Perfect.

He had no idea if the house was sitting on a shelf or had to be built. He also couldn't determine whether it would arrive in Maine in time for Christmas. For this kind of money, he wasn't taking any chances, so he called the contact number, expecting to get an answering machine. Instead, a man's voice answered. "Howard's Miniatures. Can I help you?"

"I'm online looking at your Vanderbilt house. I don't suppose you've got one ready to go?"

The man chuckled. "This must be your day. I made one for a customer who called yesterday to tell me she changed her mind. I'll knock ten percent off the price since it's not custom."

Good so far. "That's cool, but can you get it to northern Maine by Christmas Eve?"

"Sure, but it'll cost. Also, one this big ships in three crates, so you'll have to assemble it."

Nick's enthusiasm wavered at the thought of assembling anything, but he charged ahead anyway. He'd figure out the details later.

"That's okay. I'll take it." Nick fumbled on the table for his wallet and read off his credit card numbers.

"Pleasure doing business with you, Mr. McHenry. Merry Christmas."

"Merry Christmas to you, too. Thanks so much."

Thirty seconds after he hung up, Nick had a confirmation email and a link to track the shipment once it was sent. His next problem was where to store it when it arrived, but he knew one of his local friends would be willing to help him with that. As for assembling it, Ben could probably put the thing together with his eyes closed, and Nick jotted a note to talk to him about it in the morning. He wasn't used to relying on people this way, and he decided it was a definite perk of being back in Holiday Harbor.

The mantel clock downstairs chimed midnight, and Nick suddenly realized what he'd been forgetting. *Kaleidoscope.*

As close to panic as he ever got, he opened his layout program and hit "publish." The seconds ticked by at a snail's pace, and he watched the spinning wheel that showed the issue's progress onto the main site.

Every Sunday, the new issue was available for subscribers at midnight. It was usually ready hours earlier, and he'd never even come close to missing that deadline. Today he'd been enjoying himself so much, he'd almost dropped the ball. Not that he believed anyone logged in at exactly midnight to read the magazine, but still. Forgetting about it until the last minute was as close to failing as he ever wanted to get.

Once the edition was uploaded, he followed his usual process and spot-checked it online. Everything looked fine, and he finished up by skimming the new section: *Person of Interest.* He'd used the sugarplum fairy picture of Julia as a link, and clicking on it took the reader into the next installment of her story. Normally, he stopped with a visual check, but this time he went through the content again.

Re-reading it took him back through the days since he first met her that cold morning outside the bakery. He'd learned so much about her, and not just from the interviews. In that time, they'd become friends, and he'd come to admire her more than he'd have thought possible. The way she crouched down to speak to children. The generosity she showed in running her toy drive and giving her time to the pageant. The patient understanding she'd shown him since learning about Ian.

Buying her the dollhouse she'd always wanted was the most impulsive thing he'd ever done, but it felt right somehow. Closing down his computer, Nick shut off the light and lay back down. Lacing his fingers behind his head, he closed his eyes and let out a contented sigh.

For the first time in years, he found himself looking forward to Christmas.

When she'd finished tidying up, Julia looked over to find Shakespeare watching her closely. "How did I do?"

Cocking his head, he studied her for a moment before saying, "It is the east, and Julia is the sun."

"I'll take that as a thumbs-up." The sound of "It's the Most Wonderful Time of the Year" chimed in from the arm of her chair, and she picked up her phone. When she saw the caller ID, she smiled and answered the call. "Hello, you two. What a wonderful surprise."

"It's not too late there, is it?" her mother asked.

"Not a bit, but it must be four in the morning there."

"You know how these holiday events are. No one wants to be the first to leave."

Gisele Stanton was the epitome of a social butterfly, so Julia knew the long night didn't concern her in the least. Her father had been raised on a large dairy farm in Wisconsin and was more the early-to-bed-early-to-rise type. "Is Dad there, too?"

"Oh, he's lost in an argument over which version of *Don Giovanni* was better last season."

"It's always best at the Opera House in Vienna."

Mom chortled as if that should be obvious to everyone. "Of course it is, but you know how people can be when they think they're right."

"Men, you mean." Another giggle, and Julia pictured her petite mother sitting on an elegant settee in some posh ladies' salon, chattering away like a giddy teenager. "What else have you been doing?"

"Some of this, some of that. Yesterday, your father averted a crisis with the Russian ambassador's children. They wanted some special toy or other, and he gave the ambassador your card. You won't mind shipping to Moscow, will you, *pétite?*"

"Of course not. I'm happy to help."

"That's my girl. Now, tell me what you've been up to."

"Business is good, considering Toyland is still new to people. I should have that first payment to you and Dad just after the holidays."

"That's not important to us," she reminded Julia breezily. "We only want you to be happy."

"Paying you back will make me happy," Julia insisted. "You and Dad have given me more than I could ever need, and it's time for me to make my own way."

Her mother sighed but let the subject drop. "As you wish. Let's talk about something other than money."

Julia had been debating whether to tell her parents about the biography Nick was publishing, and now seemed like the time to clue them in. While she did, her mother asked several questions, most of which weren't about her, but the reporter covering the story.

"He's from Holiday Harbor, then?" she commented. "How interesting."

"And then today," Julia said as she curled up on the sofa, "you'll never guess."

After a few tries, Mom gave up with a laugh. "Enough! Tell me."

"We went sledding, then out to dinner with friends. It's the first time since I moved here that I felt like a local, like I really fit in here."

The add-on surprised her—she hadn't been aware of feeling that way until just now. It was as if talking with her cheery mother had opened up the bubbly part of Julia that had been in hiding for the past year.

"There's something else, Julia. I can hear it in your voice."

Even from thousands of miles away, her mother's intuition was infallible, and Julia laughed. "How do you always know?"

"I know my girl, that's how. This Nick McHenry is important to you, isn't he?"

"Maybe," she hedged, unwilling to go completely over the edge. "We're getting acquainted, and right now we're friends."

"Good friends."

"Yes," Julia relented with a sigh. "But please don't tell Dad. He'll call Nick and interrogate him or have him investigated by some private detective. I know he means well, but I'd rather he didn't know, at least for now."

"All right, I'll put your secret in the safe." After

a moment, she giggled. "I mean, your secret is safe with me. I still get that one wrong sometimes."

In Julia's imagination, she pictured her mother, dressed to the nines, laughing out loud as if no one else could hear her. Of all the things Julia adored about the woman who'd raised her, it was the ability to simply be herself that Julia cherished the most. Someday, she vowed, she'd regain the confidence Bernard had stolen from her and enjoy who she was again.

"The ambassador's wife just waved me over, so I should go. *Bon nuit, ma pétite.*"

Julia smiled at the familiar nighttime phrase. "*Bon nuit, Maman.* Sleep well."

After hanging up, she leaned back into the sofa cushions with a smile. This was the first time she'd told anyone about Nick, and it felt wonderful. Today had been the best day she'd had in months, and she knew it was mostly because she'd spent so much of it with him.

She'd seen a side of him instinct told her most people never got even a glimpse of. His initial wariness seemed to be fading, while his trust in her was getting stronger. That faith was crucial to her being able to reconcile him with his father, she realized. The fact that it was growing was a very good sign, but she wasn't sure it was developing fast enough.

Two weeks until Christmas Eve, she mused while she surfed through TV channels. Not much time to undo sixteen years' worth of bitterness, but she wasn't giving up just yet.

Chapter Eight

Lainie had to be at the church early Wednesday night, something about one of the wise men needing a bigger turban. Feeling generous, Nick offered to keep an eye on Hannah until rehearsal started. Fortunately, that was easy. All he had to do was sit down at the piano.

Skipping up behind him, she stopped and gazed longingly at the old upright. "I really love the way you play, Uncle Nick. It's so pretty."

Beginning the simple warm-up his mother had taught him as a child, he grinned. "It's not hard. Wanna try?"

Frowning, she held up her hands. "Aren't they too small?"

"Actually, they're just the right size." To prove it, he took them in his and placed them over the keys. She couldn't span as many notes as he did, but he showed her how to glide along and do a basic scale.

"I did it!" Clearly delighted, she gave him a gap-toothed grin. "Can you teach me a song?"

"Depends on which one you want to learn. Some are harder than others."

"'Silent Night,'" she replied instantly. "It's Mommy's favorite Christmas song."

That one I can manage, Nick thought with a grin of his own. "Sure, munchkin. Just do what I do."

Concentrating intently, she mimicked him more closely than he'd expected. She missed a couple of black keys, but when they went through it again she played it flawlessly. When he heard her humming along, he suggested, "Let's sing it, just for fun."

She was a natural with music, he thought, like Lainie. Because she wasn't wrapped up in deciphering the written notes and trying to get them right, Hannah played with an ease that amazed him. Nick was a decent pianist, and he had a fair voice, but his talent paled in comparison to his niece's.

"You're fantastic all on your own." He complimented her without reservation. "If you got some lessons with Gramma, you'd be awesome."

"Really?"

"Definitely. How 'bout we play it again?" he

suggested. "This time, I'll add in the chords while you do the melody, and we'll see how it sounds."

Partway in, another voice picked up the alto harmony line, and Nick glanced back to find his mother standing behind them. When they reached the end, she spread her arms to hug them both. "Very pretty, you two. It does this Irish heart good to hear such fine music in my family."

"Uncle Nick taught me, Gramma," Hannah informed her proudly. "He's really good."

"I had a great teacher," he added, smiling up at his mother. "Turns out, I remember more than I thought."

Beaming, she patted his shoulder in a fond gesture. "I'm so glad."

"How's Dad feeling?"

She let out an exasperated sigh. "Well enough to ignore the doctor's orders. When I left, he was outside knocking icicles off the gutters. Todd offered to do it, but your father wouldn't let him."

Nick felt a stab of guilt as his mother headed for the choir box. With the frigid weather settling in, he should've thought to help out at their place. He'd been so busy with *Kaleidoscope's* usual work and Julia's bio, it hadn't even occurred to him that his parents could use a hand. Then again, if the pastor had refused help from someone he liked, he definitely wouldn't accept it from the son he'd barely spoken to for years.

Feeling a small hand on his arm, he looked down at Hannah. "Are you okay, Uncle Nick? You look sad."

"Sometimes I wish things were different, that's all."

He hadn't meant to say that out loud, but she took it in stride. "They will be."

"You're so sure?"

"I asked God to bring you home, and you came. Tonight when you say your prayers, just ask Him for what you want."

It didn't work that way for him, but Nick wasn't about to ruin her belief in the Almighty, especially not at this time of year. Because he couldn't agree with her honestly, he went with something upbeat. "Why don't you go see if your mom's got your halo ready?"

"Okay."

After a quick hug, she hopscotched down the center aisle, completely at home in the place he'd rejected so long ago. As he watched her go, he hoped she never lost her faith.

Because once you did, it was almost impossible to get it back.

It started snowing around midnight on Wednesday.

The weather station had been issuing dire predictions all week long, but even the worst estimates proved to be optimistic compared to the reality. By Saturday afternoon, they had more than five feet of snow, with no end in sight. What had started out as a couple of snow days for the schools became a mounting crisis for the town. With temperatures in the teens and howling, relentless winds, the small fishing village was effectively cut off from the rest of the world.

But that didn't faze these sturdy folks, Julia thought as she looked down onto Main Street from her apartment. Once the plow went through, local business owners bundled against the frigid air came out with shovels, keeping the sidewalks clear and salted. Farther out, she noticed a small army shoveling out driveways for those who'd been overwhelmed by the record snowfall.

One figure in particular caught her eye, and she recognized the outfit Nick had worn when they went sledding. She was so proud of him for pitching in, she decided she needed to do something, too. Before she could decide how to help, she heard someone knocking on the outer door. Going downstairs, she was surprised to see Ben and his father, Craig, framed in the frosted-over glass.

Opening the door, she stood back to let them in. "Would you like to come in and warm up?"

"Actually, we noticed the snow on these roofs is getting pretty deep," Ben told her. "We're gonna go up and clear 'em off so they don't cave in under the snow load. Just didn't want to scare you when you hear us clomping around up there."

Frowning, she said, "Isn't that dangerous? It must be slippery."

In answer, he held up some kind of harness. "We use these when we're roofing, so we'll be fine. Don't worry—we do this whenever it snows this much. It's just our way of helping out."

That was how they did things here, she thought with a little smile. No whimpering or waiting for someone else to take care of whatever needed doing. Self-sufficient by necessity, they simply pulled on their boots and got to work. Just another quality she admired in the residents of her adopted home.

"It'd be easier to go up on this end and work our way down," Ben added. "As long as you don't mind."

"Mind?" She laughed at the very idea. "I'm grateful to you both. When you're done, stop back in and I'll have something hot for you to eat."

"Thanks very much, Miss Stanton," Craig said respectfully. "We'll do that."

"You're welcome, and it's Julia." Opening the door for them to leave, she was struck with the urge to join in some of the hard work going on. "Before you go, do you have a spare shovel? I should really get my section of the walk cleared."

"I'll do it," Ben offered.

For too long, she'd accepted that kind of help, and it had spoiled her terribly. Firmly, she shook her head. "If I'm going to be a real New Englander, I have to learn how to deal with snow."

"Good for you." Grinning, he handed her the shovel he was holding. "I've got a spare in the truck."

"Thank you." Taking it from him, she said, "I know you're pros, but please be careful up there."

When they were gone, she flipped all the lights on and turned up the gas fireplace. Normally meant for providing atmosphere, at a higher setting it put out quite a bit of heat, quickly warming the large space. Using two large poster boards, in large letters she wrote *Hot coffee and food— FREE* and hung one in each of her display windows.

She ran upstairs and brought down the trays of Christmas goodies she'd been trying to pawn off on customers. Then she started a pot of her best coffee. After that, she pulled on her boots and ski coat and started in on the portion of sidewalk that ran in front of Toyland.

Her store, she thought with pride as she tossed the first shovelful aside. In her town, where she was finally making a home for herself. After all she'd been through the past year, it felt wonderful to be settled here, in this town filled with down-

to-earth people who took care of themselves—
and their neighbors.

Not everyone had immediately accepted her as
part of the town, of course, but she'd anticipated
that. It took a while for a close-knit community
to open up and accept someone new. She understood that some never would, but she'd made several good friends and had begun creeping out of
her self-imposed shell.

Nick's skillful interviews had helped her with
that, and it hit her that she'd benefited from them
as much as he had. Pausing, she rested her hands
on the shovel handle as something occurred to
her.

She'd proposed the biography series as a way
to keep Nick in town long enough to reconcile
with his father. When she'd concocted the plan as
a gift for Lainie and her family, Julia had had no
idea that it would end up being good for her, too.

Looking up into the falling snow, she smiled.
"Thank you."

The quiet moment passed as a trio of snowmo-
biles flew down the middle of Main Street. The
teenagers riding them circled the square, parking
next to a huge puddle that had formed during the
last melt and then froze when the temperature
plummeted.

Hollering and laughing, they met up with a guy
in a pickup loaded down with two nets and all

manner of hockey equipment. Through the open cab windows, she heard something that sounded like a fusion of classic rock and rap. She didn't recognize the song, but they all sang along while they set up their hockey rink and chose teams. It was the kind of small-town scene any movie director would envy, and Julia watched them play for a few minutes.

Eventually she got back to work because she knew if the walk wasn't clear when Ben returned, he'd finish it for her. And from here on out, she was determined to be the kind of girl who took care of herself.

Ugly as they were, Nick was happy to be wearing Todd's knee-high waterproof boots and Eskimo outfit. The only part of him that wasn't covered was his eyes, and he discovered a bonus effect of the concealing wardrobe: no one knew who he was. If he didn't speak, anyone who'd written him off years ago had no clue he was one of the crew shoveling out driveways and clearing paths leading to houses that were pretty well socked in. As the six-man group he was with slowly worked their way up one side of Main Street and down the other, he couldn't help grinning. If only these grateful folks knew…

When they reached the Safe Harbor Church,

though, he quit feeling so smug. What he saw there got his temper simmering.

Front loaders had cleared the worst of the buildup, lifting it into piles over six feet high around the parking lot. The driveway of the small rectory was also clear, but that was as far as they'd gotten. Nick had no doubt that his father had sent them off to help elsewhere, assuring them he could manage the footpaths on his own.

"What do you think you're doing?" Nick demanded as he jumped from the back of Todd's old SUV and pushed his way through snow up to his waist. "Are you trying to give yourself an actual heart attack?"

"My home, my responsibility," the pastor shot back, sounding a little winded. "You boys head to the next stop. I'll be fine."

That was when Nick noticed their windows were dark. "When did your power go out?"

"Half hour ago," Dad grunted, tossing aside half a shovelful of the heavy, wet snow. "Your mother's rounding up the candles and lanterns."

"Dad, staying here doesn't make any sense. Lainie's got a gas stove and fireplace, so you'd be a lot more comfortable there. Why don't you go help Mom pack up a few things, then come home with Todd and me?"

"My parishioners—"

"Are staying put, if they're smart," Nick interrupted firmly. "But if it'll make you feel better, leave a note on the door with Lainie's phone number. Folks can call there if they need you."

Because it had come from him, Nick feared the suggestion would be thrown back in his face, and he waited to see how his pragmatic solution would fare. The two of them stared at each other, the father belligerent, the son confident he was right.

In the end, Dad was the one who blinked first. "Fine, but only because your mother needs to be warm. I'd have been just as happy staying right here."

Away from me, Nick added silently. Out loud, he forced himself to be more positive. "I'm sure she'll appreciate that. I'll shovel a path from the front door out to the driveway for you."

To his complete shock, the man who'd always had a smile for everyone else finally spared one for him. "Thank you, son."

Nick recalled the last time his father had addressed him that way—the night they rushed him to the hospital. Long pent-up emotions suddenly clogged his throat, and he swallowed hard to push them back down as the pastor went inside.

Feeling a hand on his shoulder, Nick turned to find Todd's eyes—the only thing visible—crinkled in a smile. "Nice job."

All this approval was hard for a guy like him to take, but he laughed. "Thanks."

"You do realize they're gonna have to take over your room, right?"

That hadn't occurred to him, but in the long run it didn't matter much. If the storm kept up, eventually the whole town would be in the dark, and he'd be happier in a sleeping bag next to the fireplace anyway.

When he said as much, Todd replied, "I didn't take you for the camping type."

"We camped a lot when we were kids," Nick told him as they continued shoveling. "It won't kill me to do it for a couple nights."

"Our last power failure lasted eight days."

"Huh. Guess you played a lot of Candyland."

They were both laughing when his parents joined them, each with a suitcase in hand.

"You seem to be enjoying yourselves," Mom commented with a hug for both of them. "Thank you so much for taking us in."

"Not a problem at all," Todd assured them as he shouldered his shovel. "Lainie and the kids will be thrilled to have you for company."

"I'll need a quiet place to work on this week's sermon," the pastor announced while they made their way to the car. "It's the last one before Christmas, and it's very important."

"Don't worry, Dad," Nick said as he peeled off his ski mask. "The guest room is yours and Mom's. I'll crash on the couch."

Mom opened her mouth to protest, but Nick quieted her with a look. When he opened the passenger door for her, she gave him a proud mother's smile. "That's very generous of you."

"Well, y'know, 'tis the season."

Grasping his chin, she shook his head back and forth the way she used to when he was younger. "Oh, that grin. I can't resist it."

Nick glanced over at his father, surprised to find he wasn't scowling. Not smiling, but not looking like he'd just eaten something nasty, either. Just as they were all settled in the SUV, the entire town went dark.

Nick's eyes wandered down the block to Toyland, which had been lit up like a hotel just moments before. "You think Julia's okay?" he asked Todd while they pulled onto snowy Main Street. "I mean, that bird of hers isn't exactly the cold-weather type."

"We should stop and check."

The car skidded into a spot, and Nick struggled to open Toyland's heavy door against the wind. "Julia?"

"Nick?" A circle of light bobbed toward him, and he saw her threading her way through the aisles, carrying a flashlight. "What are you doing here?"

"Do you have a generator?"

"No," she said in a dejected tone. "I will after this, though."

"You get some things together, and we'll head to Lainie's. I'll take care of Shakespeare."

While they headed upstairs, she said, "His carrier's in the closet in my office. Are you sure Lainie won't mind having such a chatty guest?"

"The kids'll love him," Nick answered confidently. "That's good enough for her."

Pausing in the dimly lit living room, Julia flashed him a grateful smile. "Thank you for thinking of us, Nick. I really appreciate it."

"No problem."

While she headed to her bedroom, Nick realized Shakespeare hadn't made a peep, which struck him as odd. A small amount of weak sunlight was still coming through the bay window, and he saw the huge bird cowering in the corner, his head buried beneath his wing.

"Hey, there, buddy." Nothing, not even a rustle of feathers. Reaching back into his college literature classes, he came up with a line from *As You Like It*. "Now we go in content."

From under the feathers came a muffled, "To liberty and not to banishment."

"Okay, then." Chuckling, Nick headed for Julia's office. "You wait here, and I'll be right back."

Five minutes later, Nick led the way back downstairs with a quilt-covered cage in one hand and a bag full of Shakespeare's food, treats and toys in the other. He belted the cage into the third row of the car, then helped Julia muscle the door of Toyland shut and lock it.

Totally spent, he collapsed into the seat next to her, and she laughed. "You really know how to show a girl a good time."

Fully aware that his parents were listening, he rolled his head to grin over at her. "Yeah, well, even us bad boys have our talents."

"Nicholas Brendan McHenry," his mother scolded. "Mind your manners."

"Yes, ma'am."

He added a wink for Julia, just to hear her laugh again. All in all, despite his aching muscles and half-frozen feet, it had been a very good day.

Even with the SUV in four-wheel drive, Todd took his time on the slick roads. The whole way out, Julia hadn't seen anything in the windows of the houses but the faintest of lights as people made do with light from fireplaces, camping lanterns and candles. Smoke trailed from every chimney, and she saw a few neighbors tramping across lawns to their friends' homes. They were greeted with open arms and laughter, and she couldn't help smiling at the thought of the friends who were welcoming her into their home. If she was going to be stranded anywhere without electricity, she couldn't ask for better hosts than the Martins.

Shakespeare hadn't made a peep since leaving her apartment, and Julia was concerned about him. At Lainie's suggestion, once they arrived at the house she set his large cage down in the warm kitchen and unzipped the heavy cover. To her dismay, one black eye glared at her accusingly from under a blue-and-yellow wing.

When she unlatched the cage door and reached inside, Nick stopped her with a hand on her arm. "You sure that's a good idea? He looks pretty mad."

"Sulking," she corrected, gently stroking the indignantly ruffled feathers on his back. "Shakespeare likes his routine, and he's not thrilled about being jerked out of his window in the dark. But you'll be warmer here," she cooed, hoping to make him feel better about the whole thing.

Untucking a little, he made a half-hearted attempt at responding. It came out like an unhappy squawk, and with a sigh she latched the door. "I guess he'll come around when he's ready."

"Julia," Lainie said, "Do you really only have one bag when Shakespeare has two plus a carrier?"

"Funny, isn't it?" she agreed with a laugh. "I wasn't sure how long we'd be here, and I wanted to make sure he has whatever he needs. Thanks so much for having us."

"No biggie," her friend assured her while she stirred a large pot of stew. "The more, the merrier."

"Smells great," Nick chimed in, dunking a piece of bread into the broth. After chewing for a few seconds, he added, "Just like Mom's."

Shoving him away from the stove, Lainie said, "It should be. She made us a triple batch last month, and I froze half of it for later. Now I'm glad I did."

Since this was her first Maine winter, the concept of laying in provisions was still as foreign to Julia as the Vienna Opera House would be for her neighbors. Sturdy and self-reliant, they apparently took their long winter in stride, preparing for the worst while they waited for spring. It had a pioneering feel to it, and she admired their upbeat pragmatism.

"That freezer downstairs is the size of my whole fridge," Nick commented as he filled a mug with fresh coffee and took a seat at the table. "You could fit a whole cow in there and then some."

"I stock up when things are on sale," Lainie explained, pulling two fresh loaves of bread from the gas oven. "If I do well enough on the budget, I can stay home 'til Noah starts school. Then I'm hoping to work as a sub so Todd and I will be off when the kids are."

"I really admire that, Lainie," Julia told her while she filled Shakespeare's water dish from a jug on the counter. "Lots of people plan their careers around how much money they can make. They forget that children just want someone to spend time with them. Kids don't care if that happens on the Riviera or in the backyard."

"Less money, more time with the kids. That's our plan."

"What about when they get older?" Nick asked. "When they want a car or to go to Harvard?"

A couple of weeks ago, the question would have irked her, thinking it was a criticism of Lainie's choices. But now, Julia noticed the twinkle in his eyes that clearly said he was just messing with his sister.

"Then we'll call Uncle Nick," she replied airily, smacking the back of his head with an oven mitt shaped like a Christmas tree. "By then, you'll be an expert at spoiling them, and we'll put it to good use."

Groaning, Nick appealed to his feathered friend. "Shakespeare, help me out here. It's two against one."

After a few seconds, the macaw lifted his head and cocked it with a wise expression. "All things in moderation."

Clearly confused, Nick looked over at Julia. "That's not Shakespeare. It's Aristotle."

His concern over her eccentric guest was touching, and she smiled. Who'd have guessed the blustery editor had such a soft heart? "Don't worry—sometimes he reverts to the Greeks when he's upset. He'll get back to the Bard when he's feeling more himself."

In the doorway, she noticed Hannah, staring at the large bird with obvious fascination. "Did he just talk?"

"He mimics people," she explained, going over to the cage. "Would you like to pet him?"

Hannah checked with her mother, who nodded her permission. Julia slid the door open and positioned her wrist for him to step onto. The macaw gave the girl a curious once-over, then apparently decided she was worth impressing and gracefully stepped onto Julia's forearm. When she drew him out, he stood up tall and shook out all his feathers in a colorful display.

Eyeing Hannah in a friendly way, he bobbed his head. "Good eve to you, milady."

Chuckling, Nick said, "How 'bout that? He likes you, munchkin."

"What did he mean?"

"That's an old-fashioned way of saying 'hello,'" Julia replied. "You should say, 'And to you, sir.'"

Hannah copied her, and the bird dipped into his

characteristic bow. When she laughed, he echoed her, and the rest of them joined in.

A few seconds later, Todd appeared in the doorway with a squirming Noah. "He was dying to get out of his jumper. I think he's afraid he's missing all the fun."

Hannah traded comments with Shakespeare, who was more than happy to oblige by repeating everything back to her. Every time he spoke, Noah squealed and let out a string of delighted giggles. It was adorable, and Julia drank in the sounds of happy children and Christmas music playing on an emergency radio in the background. She couldn't imagine a more perfect sound.

She didn't often feel lonely, but sitting here in the Martins' cozy house, it suddenly became clear what was missing from her life.

A family.

Someday, she promised herself, she'd have a kitchen like this. A place where the people she loved would gather to share news, drink cocoa and snatch treats from the counter.

Of course, there were some things she needed to do to make that dream a reality, but that didn't bother her.

God had led her to Holiday Harbor to show her the home He had in mind for her. She trusted Him to guide her down the path to where she was meant to be.

When she felt a hand on her shoulder, she looked back to find Nick standing behind her. "Maybe Hannah can watch Shakespeare while we finish up this week's interview. It's the last piece I need before posting this week's issue."

"But there's no power for the wireless router. Can you still upload to the site?"

Motioning her into the living room, he answered, "I have a gadget that taps into the cell tower and beams stuff off the satellite. At least, that's what the guy claimed when he sold it to me," he added with a wry grin.

Todd had a roaring fire going on the hearth, and Nick pulled up a couple of chairs to the warmest spot. As she sat, Julia was surprised to see him open his laptop as if a lack of power was the least of his worries. "Would you rather take notes by hand so we don't drain the battery?"

"Nah. I've got two spares and a charger that works in the car," he explained while he tapped the mouse. "We're good."

Julia considered her own response to the power failure, which had been a step short of panicking. If it hadn't been for her flashlight, she'd have been hard-pressed to navigate through her own store. "Are you always so well prepared?"

"I try to be. Being Irish, I'm well acquainted with Murphy's Law."

There was that twinkle in his eyes again. She'd

been catching it more often lately, and she wondered if there was something in particular that had improved his attitude so dramatically from the first time they'd met. Since she had no idea how to ask him something that personal without appearing to pry, she opted to keep her observation to herself. "So, where were we?"

Nick tapped up a few times to reread what they'd already covered. "The summer you spent volunteering at the reserve in Kenya."

"That's where I met Liam, Shakespeare's owner," she commented absently in an attempt to orient herself. It was harder than it sounded, reminiscing through your own life. This segment was even harder because soon she'd have to decide how to present the humiliating set of circumstances that had driven her from the glittering lifestyle she'd adored.

Or had she? Thinking back now, she couldn't recall ever being as happy as she'd been since moving to Holiday Harbor. There were problems, of course, mostly with people making unfair assumptions about her. But she was gradually winning over the residents of her adopted home, and some of them had come to feel like family to her.

"Are you still with me?" Glancing over, she saw Nick watching her intently. "Did I hit a nerve?"

"Oh, no. Just thinking."

As if sensing that this was more personal, he

closed the computer and gave her his full attention. "About what?"

She hesitated, then replied, "How to frame what happened with Bernard."

"Yeah, I've been debating that myself." Meeting her eyes, he offered a sympathetic smile. "It's up to you, but I vote we leave it out."

It was a good thing she was sitting down, or she might have collapsed from shock. Was this the same demanding, hard-edged ogre who single-handedly struck fear into the hearts of freelance reporters all over the country? "I don't understand. Don't you want to give your readers the truth?"

"No matter how much it hurts?" he added, shaking his head. "Anyone close to you knows what happened, and for strangers, it's none of their business. Trotting out the sordid details doesn't help anyone, and it would embarrass you. I think you've been through enough this past year."

"Then what will you say to explain why I came to Holiday Harbor?"

Leaning back, Nick eyed her with a thoughtful expression. She could almost hear the gears spinning in his quick mind. "You were looking for a challenge, so you chose to pull up stakes and make a new life for yourself here. Building on your love of toys, you chose to use your education and experience to take a vacant old storefront and grow it into a thriving business."

"I love it," she approved. "It leaves out the ugly part but still sticks to the truth and focuses on what's really important to me." Curious, she leaned on the arm of her chair so she could speak quietly. "What's important to you, Nick?"

She'd expected him to answer "success" or "money." To her astonishment, he slowly shook his head. "These days, I'm not sure. The past few years, starting my own magazine and making it profitable was what drove me. But now—"

He shrugged, and she filled in the blank. "You've done that, so what's next?"

"Exactly." Giving her a sheepish grin, he said, "Don't tell anyone, but I'm thinking about closing down the week between Christmas and New Year's so I can enjoy the holidays."

Reaching over, she felt his forehead. "No fever. What brought on this sudden fit of holiday cheer?"

"I don't know." Shrugging, he gave her a long, pensive look. "Maybe it's you."

For a moment, she thought he was serious. Then the glimmer in his eyes gave him away, and she laughed in relief. Much as she liked him, the last thing she needed was for him to think he was falling in love with her. She wasn't ready for a relationship, and she didn't want anything to interfere with the friendship they were developing. "Taking off for the holidays is a wonderful idea."

"You really think so?"

"Absolutely. You can use the time to work on your snowboarding."

Chuckling, he rubbed a hand over the telltale raspberry on his cheek. "Yeah, I pretty much stink."

She'd never heard him criticize his skill at anything, and she was well and truly amazed. Since Thanksgiving, some mysterious change had come over him, and the grumbly businessman she'd met that first chilly morning had morphed into someone much more relaxed. That he'd even consider closing up shop for the holiday he once claimed to hate gave her great hope for him.

"There's other things I could do, too," he suggested in a playful tone that snared her attention.

Deciding to play along, she arched an eyebrow. "Really? Like what?"

Glancing around to make sure no little ones were listening, he said, "Maybe I could spend more time with you, not taking notes. Whattya say?"

Without a single thought, she smiled. "I say that sounds like fun."

Julia knew encouraging him was foolish at best, but she simply couldn't resist that twinkle in his eyes. While they chatted, the conversation was more friendly than romantic, and she was fairly confident there was no harm in it.

Since that one errant kiss, nothing even remotely similar had happened between them. He didn't seem to be after her heart, which was good news for her. These days, it was all she had left to lose, and she intended to hang on to it for a very long time.

Chapter Nine

After finishing up his article, Nick needed to swap his dwindling battery for a fresh one from his laptop bag in the guest room. That meant interrupting his father's practice sermon, which wasn't first on his list of smart things to do.

Standing at the end of the short hallway, he stared at the closed guest room door, willing it to open on its own. A few minutes later, Lainie found him there.

"Just go knock," she suggested lightly. "He won't bite you or anything."

"You know how he is when he gets started," Nick argued. "He likes to make it all the way through."

Giving him a look that said she thought he was nuts, she asked, "You want me to go?"

Actually, that would have suited him just fine, but Nick's pride wouldn't allow her to take the heat for him. Squaring his shoulders, he replied, "If I'm not back in five minutes, send Hannah in to rescue me."

Laughing, she shook her head and continued down the stairs. It was so easy for her, Nick lamented. Dad adored his little girl, and Nick had seen firsthand how he felt about the son-in-law and grandkids she'd brought into his life. Nick knew his parents both loved him, but ever since Ian's death, he'd been certain he'd never regain his father's respect.

From the back of his mind came a thought: he'd never manage that if he was afraid to knock on a door and walk into a room.

Before he could think about it twice, he strode down the dark hallway and knocked quietly. The voices inside stopped abruptly, and he summoned a calm tone. "It's Nick. I just need to get something from my bag."

Mom let him in, her tight smile alerting him that the sermon had given way to an argument. About him, no doubt. "Come in, honey. Your father's done anyway."

Nick couldn't help glancing at the pastor, whose furious expression was as much a warning flag as hers had been. Hoping to ease the tension, he joked, "You oughta think about easing up on the fire and brimstone, Dad. You're red as a beet."

That earned him a stony glare. "I'll thank you not to tell me how to do my job, Nicholas."

"I'll thank you not to call me 'Nicholas,'" he shot back reflexively. Unfortunately, by the time he realized what he'd done, it was too late to backpedal, so he held his ground and glared back. Mom wisely left the chilly room, closing the door behind her.

"That temper of yours is going to get you in serious trouble one of these days," the pastor cautioned, pointing at him for emphasis. "'Pride goeth before a fall.'"

"Spare me your platitudes. I've heard 'em all."

"A shame none of them got through that thick skull of yours. No matter what I've said, or how I've phrased it, you choose to ignore every lesson I've tried to teach you."

The bitterness in his voice sliced into Nick's heart, and suddenly he lost the will to fight. It was as if all these years of defending himself from his father's disapproval had depleted him and he just didn't have the strength for one more battle.

"I'm sorry you're so disappointed in me, Dad. After Ian died I tried to take his place, but I don't have what it takes to compete with a ghost."

With that, Nick calmly picked up his equipment bag and left.

The living room was full of people wearing very curious expressions, but he didn't trust himself to join them without biting someone's head off. Instead, he pivoted into the kitchen, dropped his bag on the table and grabbed his borrowed jacket from its hook. It was still damp, but he didn't really care. Pulling it on, he stalked outside and put some distance between himself and the house that suddenly felt way too small.

He was so steamed, it took him a few minutes to register the fact that it had stopped snowing. Looking up into the gray sky, he caught the faint crunch of feet in the snow behind him. Assuming it was Lainie, he snarled, "I'm not in the mood."

"Obviously."

At the sound of Julia's gentle voice, he closed his eyes and sighed before turning to face her. "Sorry for snapping at you. I thought you were my nosy little sister."

"No, just your nosy friend. I thought you might want these." Smiling, she handed him a warm hat and a pair of snow gloves. "It's pretty cold out here."

That she'd thought to bring them out floored him. Accustomed to watching out for himself, her kind gesture lightened some of the weight he'd dragged outside with him.

Pulling on the gloves, he warned, "I don't wanna talk about it."

"Talk about what?"

When he glanced over at her, she gave him

an innocent look that rivaled Hannah's best. Despite his jangling nerves, he had to laugh. "You're really good at that. I can see how you managed to derail the press for so long."

"We all have our talents. For someone like me, living in the spotlight without getting burned is a survival skill." After a moment, she frowned. "My one mistake cost me everything, though."

He'd come to admire her sunny disposition, and hearing her sound so dejected just about broke his heart. "It cost you money, sure, but you still have your parents and some great friends. Lots of people would envy you, even now."

"Starting over isn't as poetic as it sounds," she corrected him gently. "You know that better than anyone."

In just a few words, she'd summed up his life since leaving Holiday Harbor, and Nick felt like he'd been hit by a truck. No one had ever spoken to him this way, and he struggled to come up with a response. "I guess." That was the best he could manage.

Those blue eyes were fixed on him, and she tipped her head in a sympathetic pose. "Are you surprised I understand how you feel?"

"Well, yeah," he blurted, "since until a few seconds ago, it didn't make sense to me."

Again, she threw him for a loop when she

laughed. "For a writer, you're sadly out of touch with your emotions."

"My staff will tell you I'm a cold-blooded editor. When I'm writing, I stick to the facts. If I wanted to deal in feelings, I'd write poetry."

"You sound like Bree when I first met her. Then Cooper taught her how to listen to her heart, and she fell in love with him. She's much happier now."

Eager to find something else to focus on, he picked up a shovel and started clearing the steps. "That's nice."

"Nick."

He tried ignoring her, but she repeated his name, more urgently this time. When he glanced over, she gave him a smile of encouragement. "Opening yourself up to joy is a good thing."

"When you open up, anything can walk in," he reminded her darkly. "Not just joy. Bad things, too."

"Wouldn't you rather take that chance than know that for the rest of your life, nothing will be any different than it is right now?"

He suspected there was another meaning hidden in her words, but he wasn't up to a philosophical discussion with someone who could probably debate in Greek. "When I take a chance, I make sure I have control over all the outcomes."

"That's not a risk. That's a sure thing. You don't get those with people."

"Bingo."

"Then you're satisfied with your life the way it is?" she pressed, clearly baffled. "There's nothing you want to improve?"

"Nope. I'm good."

That wasn't entirely true, and judging by her skeptical look, she knew it as well as he did. But it was the strategy he'd devised so he could leave his past behind and make a life somewhere else.

And he was sticking to it.

Completely at a loss, Julia finally gave up and went back inside. Nick was beyond hardheaded, to the point of hurting himself by refusing to compromise. It made absolutely no sense to her, and as she shed her winter gear, she tried to put herself in his shoes.

He was a smart guy, observant and talented. She'd noticed his softer side when he was with Hannah and his friends, and he'd certainly given Julia a glimpse into a heart that felt much more deeply than he wanted to admit. She could still hear what he'd said to his father earlier, his voice seething with a nasty mix of fury and pain.

After Ian died I tried to take his place, but I don't have what it takes to compete with a ghost.

The man she met just a few weeks ago would

never have put those feelings into words. He'd have felt them, certainly, but he'd have kept them locked away, the way he'd done for so many years. Julia couldn't imagine enduring that kind of pain in silence. She was beginning to understand how Nick had come to be the way he was. He had so much potential, but she could see why he was afraid to open up and give people the opportunity to wound him any further.

Everyone else was in the living room, and when she walked in she noticed Ann and Daniel at the end of the sofa nearest the fireplace. Daniel sat with his arms folded, staring into the flames while Ann spoke quietly to him. Her face was taut with barely restrained anger, but he refused to look at her. Stubborn as her husband, she doggedly kept at him, although her tone never rose far enough for others to hear what she was saying.

As it had with Nick, Julia's heart went out to them both. Someone had to do something, and it had to be done quickly. Once Nick returned to Richmond, he wasn't likely to make this trip again anytime soon.

"Julia, do you want to play Sorry with us?" Hannah asked.

Sitting on an inflatable camping mattress, the Martins were clustered around the game board, clearly attempting to give the McHenrys some privacy. With a sleeping Noah in her arms, Lainie flashed a worried look from her parents to Julia. Her friend's expression made it clear to Julia that things hadn't improved much since she'd gone outside.

Instinct told her that if she was going to broker peace between Nick and Daniel, it was now or never. "Maybe later. I was hoping to talk to your Grampa for a few minutes."

That got Daniel's attention, and he sent her a grateful look as he stood. "Of course. We can talk in the kitchen."

Obviously, he believed she was rescuing him from his tongue-lashing. She felt bad for the disappointment he was about to receive but pushed the regret aside to focus on what she wanted to say. From watching her father in action, she'd learned that with sensitive personal issues, the opening for making true progress could pass by in a blink.

He pulled out a chair for her, then sat opposite her and folded his hands on the table. "Now, then. What would you like to talk about?"

Patience, Julia, she reminded herself as she heard her father's voice in her memory. *People need to be led, not bludgeoned.* The subject of Daniel's last sermon popped into her head, and she sent up a silent prayer of thanks for the inspiration.

"I was wondering about the Prodigal Son

story," she began. When he nodded, she went on. "How could a father embrace a son who left the family for so long? It's never made sense to me."

Chuckling, he sounded more like the kind, understanding pastor she'd come to know the past few months than the rigid man refusing to listen to his wife. "Lots of folks have that problem. The story isn't really about the young man but the father. He was wise enough to allow his son to leave, then welcomed him home, pleased that he'd come back to the family on his own terms."

"I see," she said, nodding. "It means more that way, doesn't it? When someone's gone for a while, it gives us a chance to miss them and appreciate what makes them who they are. Then when we see them again, we have the perspective we need to forgive them their mistakes, whether we agree with their choices or not."

"I suppose that's one way of looking at it."

Judging by his suddenly guarded expression, she knew she'd hit a nerve. Not a bull's-eye, but close enough that hc was suspicious of her motives for starting this conversation. There was no turning back now, so she gathered her courage and charged ahead. "Did you ever try that with Nick? Forgiving him, I mean."

Looking sullen, he held her gaze as if daring her to continue. Apparently, Nick shared more of his father's attributes than she'd realized. Instinct told her it was time to be direct. "Nick blames himself for Ian's death. Do you feel the same way?"

Daniel opened his mouth, then slowly let it close. Pain replaced the anger in his eyes, answering her more eloquently than any words ever could have. "I tried not to," he confessed quietly. "But I'm ashamed to say it was a struggle for me."

Sharp as he was, she was certain Nick had picked up on Daniel's conflicting emotions, which had only added to his own sense of guilt. No wonder their relationship had degraded so badly over the years. "What about Ann?"

"Never," he replied instantly, shaking his head for emphasis. "She accepted God's will much more easily than I did."

"And I imagine it didn't help that Ian wanted to stay here and take over your church while Nick couldn't wait to leave Holiday Harbor."

"I never understood it," he said, clearly still bewildered all these years later. "They were like night and day, those two. Ann, Lainie and I love this town and the people who live here. Nick couldn't wait to get away from it. From us," he added in a miserable tone.

"But he came back for Thanksgiving," she pointed out as kindly as she could. "That must mean something."

"It means Ann and Lainie shamed him into coming. Nothing more."

"They're happy to have him, and Hannah's enjoying getting to know him." Pausing, she let Daniel absorb that before bringing down the hammer. "Are *you* glad to see him?"

"You can't possibly understand," he hedged. "It's complicated."

Hoping to ease his anxiety, she smiled. "I don't think it is. He and I have talked quite a bit, and I think he's ready to put the past behind him. The question is, are you willing to do the same?"

"I—"

"What do you think you're doing?"

Startled by the sharp voice behind her, Julia whipped around to find Nick standing in the doorway. Fury rolled off him in waves she could feel from several feet away. "I was talking with your father."

"About something that's absolutely none of your business."

"So you dissecting my personal life for anyone with a magazine subscription is fine," she shot back, "but I can't discuss yours with your own father?"

"That's different, and you know it." He turned to the pastor, and his expression softened with honest concern. "Dad, this is between you and me. You don't have to go through it with her."

"All right." Standing, Daniel said, "I think I'll go see what your mother's doing."

Once he was gone, Nick turned on Julia with blazing eyes. "The man has a heart condition, and here you are stressing him out. Are you trying to give him a heart attack?"

Though he tried to appear distant and cool, this wasn't the first time she'd witnessed his protective streak. It probably ran deeper than even he realized, and it made her tread carefully. "Of course not. I'm trying to help relieve some of the strain he's under by getting him to see things from your perspective. Which I got from you, by the way."

He pointed an accusing finger at her. "That was a private conversation. I didn't think you'd be careless enough to repeat it to anyone, especially not my father."

"Careless?" While she understood he was upset with her for meddling, she couldn't allow his biting accusation to slip by unchallenged. Rising from her seat, Julia drew herself up to her full height the way she'd learned during years of ballet classes. The posture put her nearly level with him, and she drilled him with an unyielding glare. "Your family made a place for me before anyone else here even bothered to find out I'm not the spoiled rich girl they see on the news. I love them as much as I do my own parents, and I'd never do anything to hurt them. I only want to help them—and you."

"Well, I got news for you, your highness. It's my life, and I like it fine just the way it is."

With that, he spun and stormed out, slamming the door behind him. He'd run through the last ounce of sympathy she possessed, and Julia was so angry, she didn't even watch him go.

She was just glad he was gone.

More livid than he'd been in recent memory, Nick stayed outside shoveling until the walks and entire driveway were clear. The good news: by the time he was ready to go back inside, everyone else was in the living room either dozing or reading. The bad news: there was nothing to eat. During his visit, he'd gotten used to Lainie leaving a note on the table for him when he was late, telling him she'd left his dinner in the fridge.

Tonight, no note. Even the tea kettle, which had been running nonstop throughout the storm, was cold. He sensed movement in the doorway and glanced over to find Todd staring at him with sympathy. "You really did it this time."

"Whatever." Shrugging, Nick grabbed an apple from the bowl on the counter and took a bite. "I'm used to it."

"From Lainie?"

"Well, no," he had to admit. "She usually takes my side."

"Not today." When Nick started to protest, Todd raised his hands. "This is your family's business, and it's not my place to step into this mess. Just thought I'd warn you."

Sadly, Nick knew that was the best he could hope for right now. When Todd retreated the way he'd come in, Nick realized he'd blundered over a line he never should have crossed. His family adored Julia, which he totally understood. She was kind and generous, and she clearly thought the world of them all.

Except for him, he acknowledged with a sigh. Over the past few weeks, he'd gotten dangerously close to falling for the remarkable woman who'd so unexpectedly crossed his path. But their argument had clearly ruined things between them— and turned his family against him. Knowing he'd get an icy reception by the fire, he opted for the less personal cold he'd find upstairs.

If he was honest, he thought as he trudged up to Todd and Lainie's room, he'd started imagining what it would be like to stay in Holiday Harbor and forge an honest-to-goodness relationship with Julia. Take her to dinner, or drive over to Oakbridge for a movie. It didn't fit with any of the plans he'd made for his life but he'd started to think it might be worth trying all the same. None of that would happen now, he recognized as he stretched out fully dressed on the bed and pulled the chilly covers over him. Furious as he'd been earlier, it had begun to dawn on him that Julia had done her best to convince him to bury the past and move forward, to the point of enlisting his father to help her make it happen.

Why did it matter so much to her? he wondered, threading his fingers together behind his head. He sifted through several ideas, but when he finally drifted off, he was no closer to an answer.

A few hours later, he woke to light piercing his eyelids. Cracking one of them open, he saw the lights had come back on, and the alarm clock display was flashing 12:00. Weak sunlight was coming through the windows, making the icicles sparkle like clear Christmas lights. With a low groan, the furnace kicked on, and the registers started pumping warm air into the chilly room. Nick picked up his phone to see that it was after six, and the internet icon was spinning at full power.

He could hear people shifting around downstairs, then the back door open and close. Now that he'd gotten some peace and quiet, he realized that staying here so long had been a horrible idea. A couple of extra days after Thanksgiving would have been enough, and then he'd have been gone before things went south with Julia. They would have parted as friends, and he'd have a collection of good memories rather than the mixed bag he'd ended up with.

There was no help for it now, so he shook off his regrets and opened his travel link. Scrolling through, he found several possible flights back to Richmond. Because of the storm, airport traffic was delayed, but he could probably leave Tuesday. Even if he had to wait another night, he'd rather do that in a Rockland hotel than here.

While he was considering which flight and hotel to book, his email alert chimed. The dollhouse maker in California was letting him know that despite the storm, his order had just touched down in Portland, Maine. It was being loaded on a truck and should be delivered by Wednesday, two days before his Christmas Eve deadline.

Julia's gift.

He'd forgotten all about it. Resting the phone against his forehead, Nick recalled that day when he'd placed the order with jumbled emotions. One of the best in his life, he'd made the mistake of allowing himself to believe it was the start of what could be a new beginning with his family, with the town…and with her. He'd taken a leap and followed his heart, making a purchase he never should have considered.

Then again, the dollhouse was going to Ben's place for him to put together and load onto his pickup. He was perfectly capable of taking it to Julia himself. Almost immediately, Nick rejected that as a cop-out. The gift was from him, and he should be the one to give it to her. The night he'd found it, he'd envisioned her reacting to it like a kid who's been surprised on Christmas morning. In truth, he'd imagined getting a delighted smile, maybe even a kiss as a reward for being so thoughtful.

The trouble was, with the way things had ended between them yesterday, she was just as likely to cut him down with some wilting remark and stroll away.

While he made the bed, he had to admit he wouldn't blame her for shutting him out. Now that his temper had cooled, he accepted her comment about wanting to help his family—and him. She'd intentionally pushed his most sensitive button, but that was no excuse for the way he'd turned on her. She'd interfered out of kindness and the desire to make things better. He'd retaliated out of—what?

Fear.

The answer came through as if someone had said it out loud, startling him so thoroughly, he sank down onto the half-made bed. The problem was, he had no clue what frightened him so much that he'd rather keep battling with his father than make amends and bring the family some peace.

He wasn't an idiot—Nick recognized that most

people found him difficult to deal with. He was demanding, and he made sure things got done his way. A perfectionist, Mom used to say. Like his father.

And in that moment, it all made sense. They were nearly identical in their approach to things, but they applied their considerable energy to vastly different goals. Because of it, they grated on each other's nerves. While Ian's death was a tragedy that had devastated them both, it wasn't the cause of their ongoing struggle.

They'd done it to themselves.

Thinking back, Nick recalled many terse lectures about his lack of commitment to God and how following his own map would lead him absolutely nowhere. He couldn't imagine how Dad felt when he rocketed from one journalism position to another, finally landing an opportunity to start his own magazine. With every success, he'd proved his father wrong, adding fuel to the fire that had simmered between them for as long as he could remember.

Contrary to what he'd believed all these years, the problem wasn't that Nick wasn't Ian. It was that he wasn't Daniel.

The revelation hit him like a bolt of lightning, driving Nick to his feet. Hurrying downstairs, he pulled up short when the conversation in the kitchen stopped abruptly. Everyone was sitting around the table, looking guilty.

Except for Hannah, who piped up, "Good morning, Uncle Nick. Mommy's making pancakes. Would you like some?"

Since Lainie was avoiding his gaze, he settled for smiling at the little girl who'd used a Christmas wish to bring him home. "I'd love some, munchkin. But save mine for me while I talk to Grampa."

"Okay." Her pink-ribboned ponytail bobbed while she nodded, and if he hadn't known better, he'd have thought she called him out on purpose. The idea that his four-year-old niece would step up for him that way made him feel a lot better than he had earlier.

"Dad?" Motioning him into the living room, Nick caught the apprehensive look that passed between his parents. Hoping to ease their minds, he added, "It's not bad, I promise. In fact, I think it'll make us all really happy."

More confident, his father stood and Nick respectfully stepped aside to let him go first. They both remained standing, their usual approach so each could make a quick exit if necessary. Nick hoped that soon they'd be able to sit and chat like a normal father and son.

"I was upstairs thinking about yesterday," he began gently. "That conversation was between you and Julia, and I shouldn't have reacted the way I did. I'm sorry if I upset you."

He'd expected a simple nod, which was the usual response when he screwed up and apologized. Instead, he got a slight smile. "I'm sorry, too. Julia's heart was in the right place, but I should've had that talk with you, not her."

The admission threw Nick off his stride, but he recovered and plowed ahead. "I appreciate that, Dad. But I have to give her credit—she got me thinking."

While he described his early morning epiphany, understanding slowly made its way across the pastor's weary features. By the time Nick was finished, those dark eyes were sparkling with something he didn't see very often: pride.

"I've never thought of it that way, but you're right," Dad acknowledged in a pensive tone. "We're both dedicated to what we do, and we have a hard time viewing things from another perspective. But I want to correct one error in your assumptions."

Delivered in the fatherly tone he used with parishioners seeking his advice, only a few hours ago the comment would have set Nick's hackles on edge. Now, it made him smile. "What's that?"

"I never expected you to become a pastor simply because that was my path. All I wanted was for you to love and honor God, to have a faith that would guide you through whatever life you chose."

Gratitude clogged Nick's throat, and he swallowed hard to keep his voice steady. "Thanks, Dad. I know we don't always agree on things, so that means a lot to me."

"We may see things differently," he said, resting a hand on Nick's shoulder. "But I'm still very proud of what you've accomplished." He could have left it there, ending their encounter with kind words instead of a slamming door. But he went on with a somber look. "Julia told me you still blame yourself for Ian's death. You'll have to make your own peace with that, but in my mind, it was nothing more than a tragic accident. I love you, and I know you'd never intentionally have done anything to harm your brother."

As if that wasn't enough, then he did something Nick couldn't have imagined in his wildest dreams. Smiling, he opened his arms in a welcoming gesture no one with a heart could resist. Nick went into that hug as a rush of unfamiliar emotions threatened to overwhelm him. He couldn't begin to describe what he was feeling, and then the perfect phrase bubbled to the surface.

"I love you, too, Dad."

Chapter Ten

Julia had anticipated that things would be off-kilter at Toyland because of the storm, but she hadn't expected anything like this. Even before opening on Sunday, two delivery trucks pulled up outside, and their drivers began unloading shipments of new stock that had been delayed by the storm. She quickly ran out of space in the store room, so as much as she hated to clog up her display area, she had no choice but to have them stack boxes out front.

She was glad Lainie had kept Shakespeare because after being uprooted from her apartment, all the commotion would probably have sent him into shock. He was one of the more intelligent creatures she'd ever come across, so she could imagine him being upset by too much upheaval. Then he'd need a bird psychiatrist, and she had no idea where to find one of those.

The absurd thought made her laugh, and she shook her head at her own foolishness. She hadn't slept well during the blackout, and she was a little loopy this morning. The deluge of toys hadn't helped any. When the jingle bells on the front door rang, without looking up she said, "I'm sorry. We're not ready for customers just yet."

"How 'bout apologies?"

She glanced up to find Nick standing in front of her, a bakery box in one hand and a rack of coffees in the other. Drawn by the scent of goodies, her assistants swooped in, gushing their thanks before disappearing into the storeroom again. For her part, Julia kept on working. She wasn't one to hold a grudge, but Nick had stepped way over the line yesterday. Being human, she wasn't above letting him sweat a little.

After several awkward seconds, he sighed. "Julia, I feel awful about yesterday. You were trying to help, and I bit your head off. I really am sorry."

"Apology accepted," she said tersely. "Thank you for stopping by."

Setting what remained of his peace offering on the counter near the register, he said, "I wanted you to know you got through to me. I was mad at first, but later on what you said made sense. This morning, Dad and I got some things out in the open that've been bottled up for a long time. We still have some work to do, but we made a good start."

Julia felt her heart beginning to soften and sternly reminded herself that this man had lashed out at her like a cobra only a few hours ago. Still smarting from the experience, she didn't want Nick to know how she was feeling right now. Hoping to keep her emotions under wraps, she busied herself arranging a fleet of construction vehicles on an empty shelf. "I'm glad to hear that."

"I don't know if you've noticed," he continued, "but once I make up my mind about something, it's kinda hard to change."

She felt a smile flickering and forced herself not to look over at him. "I've noticed."

Apparently, he'd had enough of her fencing, and he boldly stepped in front of her, blocking her from the shelves. "Not everyone has what it takes to make me see things from another perspective. I really appreciate you not giving up on me."

He didn't touch her, but the warmth glowing in his eyes reached deep inside her to a place she knew would always belong to him. Despite her best efforts, somehow she'd become very fond of this arrogant, aggravating man who had a knack for making her smile.

Giving in to the impulse, she did just that as she gazed up at him. "You're very good at apologizing."

"Lots of practice," he admitted, cocking his head in an uncertain gesture. "Does that mean you forgive me?"

She laughed. "It's Christmas. How could I not?"

Relief flooded his features, and he drew her into his arms for a long, emotional embrace. Burying his face in her shoulder, he murmured, "Thank you."

"You're welcome." As she pulled away, his hesitant expression gave way to an admiring grin, and she decided there was nothing she enjoyed more than seeing this very intense man smile. "I hate to do this, but between catching up with stock and sending out orders, we're crazed in here. I really have to get back to work."

"I could help," he replied immediately, tossing his coat on the counter. "What do you need?"

Ordinarily, she'd politely tell him it wasn't necessary, but today was a different story. An extra pair of hands would make all the difference, and she was more than grateful for his offer. "We open in an hour, and I'd really like to have the shop floor clear when customers start coming in. If you can stock out here, I'll start on the shipping."

"You got it, boss." He made an odd face, and they both laughed. "That sounds weird. Usually, other people say that to *me*."

"Don't worry. I'll just pretend I didn't hear it."

On her way past him, she patted his shoulder in a friendly way. To her surprise, he caught her hand and reeled her close enough that for a moment, she thought she was in for another kiss. Instead, he simply looked down at her, dark eyes glittering with blatant admiration. His heart beat a comfortable rhythm under her palm, a sensation so intimate she almost forgot to breathe.

"I've never met anyone like you," he finally said in a voice barely above a whisper. "Gorgeous, smart and sweet, all wrapped up in one amazing package."

"I—" Blinking up at him like a mindless twit, she finally found some words. "Thank you."

"You're welcome."

Flashing her one of his most maddening grins, he brushed his lips across the back of her hand, then released it and sauntered away to start restocking the art supplies.

Julia stood there for a full minute, waiting for her heart to stop running away with her. She could feel the heat in her cheeks and took several deep breaths to regain her usual composure. She'd known her share of intelligent, sophisticated men from all over the world, she mused as she went to the computer and pulled up her shipping list. Why on earth did this smart-aleck editor drive her to distraction?

Her romantic mother would have a quick answer to that one. With a delighted smile, she'd inform her very pragmatic daughter that she was in love with Nick McHenry. Only one problem: it was a horrible idea. They were opposites in every way, and while Julia could imagine that working for other couples, she wasn't sure about it for herself.

Then again, he'd told her he was considering closing down his business so he could enjoy the holidays. The driven businessman she'd met after Thanksgiving detested Christmas and couldn't wait to leave his charming hometown behind.

What had changed? she wondered as she boxed up an order of train accessories. If Nick's confession was sincere, she'd found a way through his tough exterior to the good heart he was hiding under all that bluster. That was all well and good, but there was one more sticking point for her, and there was no getting around it.

Nick had rejected his faith long ago. She understood the reason, even sympathized with it to an extent, but it was a major obstacle to any kind of relationship. Over the past year, she'd had lots of time to examine her past failures with romantic relationships, and while the men were as different as could be, they all had one thing in common.

None of them shared her faith. It was such an important part of her life, not just for the community at church but as a beacon that guided her every day. Despite the recent knocks she'd taken, Julia recognized that she'd led—and continued to lead—an exceptional life. That was no accident, and she was grateful to God for keeping watch over her.

By helping with the pageant, Nick had taken a few tentative steps back toward the right path, but he still had a long way to go. Much as she cared about him, she knew that until he made his peace with God, there was no future for them.

Julia would help him all she could, but in the end it was up to him.

Wednesday afternoon, Nick was out fetching critical packing supplies for Julia when his phone rang. Seeing Ben's face on the screen, he answered with a desperate, "Please tell me the dollhouse is at your place."

"Just got here, all three crates of it." When he chuckled, Nick was reminded that Ben was so laid-back, he made easygoing Cooper look tense. "This thing is enormous, man. It really should be built wherever Julia wants to have it. Like forever—because once it's put together, there won't be any good way to move it."

Nick frowned at the unanticipated complication. Until now, the biggest obstacle had been getting the large house delivered in time for Christmas. As his mind raced for a solution, he pictured her large, empty living room and the vacant space between two built-in bookcases that had once held some kind of wide cabinet. He was pretty good with measurements and described the spot to Ben.

"That'd work, I think. I'd hate to put it on the floor, though. I've seen that collection of hers, and she'll want it up where she can see everything."

"There's a long antique table in her upstairs office. You can use that for a base."

"Okay, but I'm gonna need some help. And how'm I supposed to get in there without anyone seeing me?"

"I borrowed a key from one of the shop assistants. They're closing at six on Christmas Eve, and we'll be out delivering gifts from the Gifting Tree, so you can go up then. How long will it take you?"

"Twenty minutes, tops. Wait a sec. Did I hear you say *you're* gonna be out delivering gifts? Isn't that against the Scrooge code?"

"Don't push it, dude."

"Okay," Ben agreed with a laugh. "Dad and I'll

get to Toyland just after six. When we're done, I'll find you at the church and let you know how it went."

"Just make sure you're cool about it, or Julia will get suspicious. And thanks, Ben," he added with feeling. "I really appreciate this."

Nick could almost hear his old buddy grinning. "You're going to an awful lotta trouble to surprise her. I think it's real nice."

"Yeah, well, she's worth it."

After they hung up, Nick took his bags into Toyland. Things were much calmer than they'd been when he left, and he looked around for something to do.

"Please, go," Julia urged, pushing him toward the door. "I know you've got a deadline, and we're fine here."

"Are you sure? I mean, I can break down boxes or something."

"You've done more than enough. Thank you for everything this week, Nick. We never could've managed without you."

"Does this mean you're free for dinner?"

Laughing, she shook her head. "We just got another delivery, so the storeroom is a disaster, and I have to get things organized by morning. I'll be working very late, so I'll take a rain check."

There was no way he was letting her choke down a sandwich and slave away half the night by herself. "I'll get takeout from The Albatross and come give you a hand. Around eight?"

The grateful look on her face was all the thanks he needed. "Perfect. I'll see you then."

Out on the sidewalk, Nick looked around the village he couldn't wait to escape from just a few weeks ago. With fluffy snowflakes coming down, everything looked bright and inviting. The twinkle lights strung everywhere gave the windows a festive look, and the garlands draped around the gazebo were dusted with snow. A shout called his attention to the hockey game in the square, and he watched several kids riding their sleds down the side of a tall snow pile on the far side of the rink.

As he got into his car, it struck him how strange it was that a scene that would have felt so hokey when he first arrived now made him smile. Holiday Harbor was one of those places that never changed, and he'd always considered that a flaw. Now, he saw it as a strength, something that kept this town— and these people—grounded and real.

On his way out to Lainie's, he passed the cobblestone wall that surrounded a spot he hadn't seen in a very long time. The bronze marker was tarnished from years out in the weather, but the raised letters were still easy to read.

Holiday Harbor Cemetery.

Stopping in the middle of the road, he stared at the sign while images of his last visit flooded his memory. He remembered standing in the shade of an oak tree, holding a sobbing Lainie, trying to be stoic while one of his father's friends droned on and on about gracefully accepting God's will. The funeral had been sixteen years ago, but sitting outside those gates, he could picture it as clearly as if it had happened last week.

Next thing he knew, Nick found himself turning onto the gravel drive, following the curve that led out toward the newer sites. After hesitating a few moments, he gathered his nerve and got out of the car. Cleared paths snaked around the gravestones, and he followed one until he got to the large McHenry plot.

His grandparents were buried there, along with some elderly relatives whose names he barely recognized. As he crunched through the deeper snow, he was aware of his steps slowing down. But eventually he landed where some inexplicable urge had compelled him to go. Pausing in front of the marker, he brushed away the snow covering the inscription.

Ian Patrick McHenry. Beloved child of God.

Nick hadn't been here since that day. Crazy as it was, he got the feeling that someone had placed a hand on his shoulder, thanking him. It was as if Ian had been waiting all this time for his little brother to come and acknowledge his resting place.

For years he'd done everything he could to erase Ian's death from his memory so he could get on with his life. Finally, Nick understood why his attempts to put the past behind him had failed so miserably. Grief-stricken and overcome by guilt, he'd reduced Ian to a single tragic moment in time, ignoring all the other things that made him who he was. Smart. Funny. The best junior hockey goalie within fifty miles.

Standing there in the frosty air, face to face with the grief he'd denied for so long, Nick realized that in trying so hard to forget his big brother's death, he'd lost sight of the life that had come before it.

As it had earlier with his father, all the fight drained out of him. Resting his hands on the unyielding stone, he sank to his knees in the snow. "I'm sorry, Ian. So, so sorry."

Around eight, Julia was in her maze of a storeroom, listening to Christmas music while she sorted through her remaining stock. Somehow, all the shipments had gone out today, but more had come in during the afternoon. The storm had put folks behind on their shopping, and today Toyland had logged its best sales all year. With only two business days left until Christmas, she was anticipating a rush of last-minute customers and overnight orders. And of course, there was the Gifting Tree.

Aaron Coleman's PR campaign had been a huge success, and the pile under the tree was enormous. At first, she'd wrapped donations as they came in, tagging each one for delivery later this week. Now it was all she could do to tack on the proper snowflake, assuring herself she'd catch up on the details later. Of course, that was before the storm.

She'd toyed with the idea of paying one of her part-timers to handle it, but if she did that, it would eat into her profits. As a new business, Toyland was doing fairly well, but she knew the black ink she'd gotten from the boost of Christmas season wouldn't last. If she was going to repay her parents' loan, she had to watch every dollar she spent.

Trusting that it would all work out in the end, she got back to her inventory. When her cell phone began singing, she nearly jumped out of her skin. The caller ID told her it was Nick, and she put it on speaker so she could continue working. "Hi, there. What can I do for you?"

"Where are you? I've been banging on this door for five minutes, and folks are starting to stare like I'm some kinda wacko."

"I'm sorry!" Glancing up at the large clock, she saw it was ten after eight. "I'm in the storeroom with the radio on so I didn't hear you. I'll be right there."

When she saw him, she actually stopped in the middle of her shop and gawked. In one hand, he held a large bag with The Albatross logo on it. Over his other shoulder he was carrying a tall pine tree wrapped in netting that did little to disguise how full it was. It must be heavy, she realized, and she hurried over to open the door.

Framed against the snowy backdrop, he grinned. "Merry Christmas."

"Merry Christmas," she replied automatically as he set the tree down. "Where on earth did you find one that big so close to Christmas?"

"In Turnberry." When she cocked her head, he said, "It's fifty miles away, and I had to cut it myself."

"You cut a tree down by yourself?" she echoed in disbelief. "I thought you were a wreath-on-the-door kind of guy."

"Yeah, well, I'm just full of surprises. If you take the food up, I'll go get the ornaments from my car and meet you upstairs."

"Nick, that's sweet, but I can't stop working right now. I'd welcome your company, but I have to get organized for tomorrow."

"A half hour won't make much difference. Especially if I stay and help."

Touched by the thoughtful offer, she shook her

head. "I'll be at this most of the night. I couldn't ask you to stay that long."

"If I stay, you'll only be at it half the night." His eyes drifted to the mound of toys under the Gifting Tree. "I'm no good with paper and ribbons, but I can handle the inventory while you wrap."

When she began to protest, he silenced her with a stern look that quickly changed her mind, making her say, "You're determined to hang around, aren't you?"

"Yup. I can either harass you the whole time or I can help. You choose."

There was that McHenry stubborn streak again. Only this time, he was using it to make her life easier, not harder. She could get used to that, she thought with a smile. "All right. Thank you."

"No problem. I'll lock the door when I've got everything inside. See you upstairs."

Deciding there was nothing to do but go along, Julia headed up to her apartment. Tonight, it felt like there were twice as many steps as usual, and by the time she reached the top, her feet were really dragging. As she rounded the banister, no one greeted her with some Elizabethan quote, and she made a mental note to pick up Shakespeare tomorrow. Nutty as he was, she missed her colorful guest.

She snapped on the few lights she'd installed and set up their meal on the coffee table. Nick had been smart enough to order sandwiches and salads along with soda for each of them. With nothing to warm up, she sat down for the first time in hours.

Next thing she knew, someone was gently shaking her awake. When her eyes drifted open, she blinked over at Nick. "Hmm?"

"I'd let you sleep, but you don't look all that comfortable. Are you hungry?"

"Mm-hmm." When she moved, her neck protested, and she rubbed it with a groan. Yawning, she confessed, "I've never been so tired in my life."

"How'd it go after I left?"

"Traffic was fairly steady all afternoon. It's nice to see people back in town after the storm, and I'm sure the other businesses did well, too."

"Have you had time to figure out your profits yet?"

After a bite of salad, Julia replied, "My hunch is we're doing well, but I won't know until I sit down and crunch the numbers later this month. Speaking of business, what did you decide about *Kaleidoscope*?"

"The last issue for this year goes out tomorrow, then nothing 'til New Year's Day. I posted the notice today, so the readers will know."

"And how did that feel?"

"Weird, but good," he confided with a grin.

"Can't remember the last time I took this much time off from anything."

And after that? Julia wanted to ask. He had a life in Richmond, completely separate from hers here in Maine. He had a condo, and a car, maybe even a plant or two. When he returned to all that, she'd miss him terribly. As rough a start as they'd gotten off to, she'd come to adore the gruff editor who claimed to hate the holidays but drove a hundred miles roundtrip to buy her a Christmas tree.

If she asked him about his plans, she feared he'd interpret that as pressure to stay. He'd already been in town three weeks longer than he'd anticipated, and she wouldn't dream of asking for more. But if he decided to stick around on his own, she certainly wouldn't complain. The last obstacle between them was still his struggle with his faith, but she was sure she could help him with that, if he'd just give her the chance.

Unwilling to spoil their cozy evening, she shoved her brooding aside, determined to make the most of the time they had left together. They continued chatting while they ate, and Julia felt some of the tension easing from her body. Resting her head back, she noticed the tree Nick had set up in an empty spot next to one of her bookshelves. The lights were strung, and boxes of ornaments sat around it, ready for hanging.

Rolling her neck, she looked over at him. "I

thought I just nodded off, but you had time to put the lights on."

Shrugging, he sipped some of his drink. "You were pretty wiped out, so I got the boring part done ahead of time. Dad used to do that when we were kids so we wouldn't drive him nuts while he was untangling the cords."

She laughed, and then she understood there was more to that comment than she'd heard at first. Raising her head, she shifted to look him in the eyes. "This is the first tree you've done on your own, isn't it?"

"I hate Christmas, remember?" Despite the sarcasm, she saw the hesitance in his expression.

"I do remember," she said gently. "What changed your mind?"

She expected him to laugh it off with some witty remark. Instead, his eyes held hers with a blazing intensity she'd never seen from anyone.

"You, Julia," he murmured. "You changed my mind. About a lot of things," he added in a pensive tone.

No posturing, no bluster, just a straightforward confession. It was so unlike him, she was completely floored. "Like what?"

Tracing the curve of her cheek with his knuckle, he smiled. "Twinkle lights. Snow. Christmas wishes. I know it sounds crazy, but earlier today

I was thinking if Hannah hadn't asked for me to come home, I never would've met you."

He had a point, and Julia easily returned the smile. "So you believe now?"

"More than I did. Decorating this tree oughta finish me off." Standing, he offered her a hand up. "Forgot to mention there's mistletoe in that bag. I asked for something simple, but the clerk insisted on selling me something called a kissing ball."

Going over to the pile of decorations, she lifted out a fragrant ball of pine, mistletoe and burgundy velvet ribbons. "Nick, it's gorgeous! Since you went to all that trouble, we'll have to find just the right spot to hang it."

Taking it from her, he looped the ribbon over a hook protruding from the wall. Flashing her a wicked grin, he reeled her into his arms. "How's that?"

"I guess we should try it out and see how it works." After a long, knee-weakening kiss, she smiled. "Perfect."

Refreshed from her nap, she enthusiastically dug into the bags and pulled out boxes of ornaments. Some were frosted, some clear, others swirled like colorful candy canes. The star was made of crystal, and she carefully set it aside so it wouldn't be crushed. "I'm amazed you could find so many nice ornaments this close to Christmas. You must have gone to every store around."

"It took a while, but I actually had fun picking everything out. It's always bugged me how downstairs was done up like Christmas central, and there was nothing up here for you."

"It's a wonderful surprise," she approved, handing him a handful of baubles ready to go. "Thank you."

"You're welcome." Looking up, he hung the decorations on some higher branches. Completely out of the blue, he said, "I went to see Ian today."

Stunned, Julia lost hold of the red ball in her hand and quickly reached for it before it could roll under the sofa. The revelation was so unexpected, it took her a few seconds to form an appropriate response. "What made you decide to go there?"

He shrugged, avoiding her gaze as he hunkered down to get some more ornaments. "I was driving past the cemetery, and something made me go in."

She knew what that something was, and her pulse leapt with joy. But she wanted to hear him say it, so she nudged. "What do you think it was?"

"It was time." He slanted a look at her and for a few moments, they just stared at each other. Finally, he relented with a deep sigh. "Fine. It might have had something to do with God leading me in that direction. Satisfied?"

She was ecstatic, but she kept her expression neutral. "That doesn't matter. Are you happy?"

"Yeah." Gradually, a smile lightened his features. "I know he's not really there, but it felt good to talk to my big brother again, y'know?"

"I do know." Julia grasped his hand for an encouraging squeeze. "What did you say?"

"I apologized." When she opened her mouth, he stalled her with a hand in the air. "Not for the accident. I know he doesn't blame me for that. I wanted him to know I was sorry for trying to forget about him. I thought it would make things easier to take, but it actually made them worse, for me and everyone else."

"You should be very proud of yourself. This is an amazing leap for you after all these years."

"I didn't make it on my own," he murmured with a grateful look. "You pushed and prodded 'til I got there. I didn't make it easy for you, and I really appreciate you not giving up on me."

How could she let this wonderful, aggravating man go back to Virginia? On the verge of telling him how she felt, Julia managed to stop herself before she blurted out something they might both regret. Instead, she smiled and said, "You're welcome."

Chapter Eleven

"You really had to deliver these on Christmas Eve?" Nick grumbled while he and Julia stacked piles of gifts in the back of Todd's SUV. He'd laid the backseat down, but by his estimation it would still be a tight fit to get everything in one load. "Couldn't these parents figure out how to hide 'em for a few days?"

"That's not the arrangement," she insisted in a gentle but firm tone that clearly said there was no wiggle room on this one. "This way, their children's presents go straight under the tree, with no time for shaking and guessing."

"Yeah, kids can be really annoying with that. When we were growing up, Lainie was the worst."

"Patience isn't her strong suit, even now."

Opening the door to go back in the shop, he motioned her ahead of him. "Wait 'til she finds out I bought her a generator."

"You didn't!" When he nodded, she laughed. "She wanted a spa weekend at that new resort. You're a dead man."

"Sure, 'til the next time the power goes out. Then I'll look like a genius."

"I'm getting one as soon as things settle down after the holidays," Julia commented while she piled more packages in his outstretched arms. "That way, Shakespeare and I can stay here during a blackout instead of imposing on Lainie and Todd."

"Aw, they loved having you there," he told her from behind his armload. "You and that crazy bird of yours were a big hit."

She lifted a smaller pile and went ahead to hold the door for him. "That's sweet, but if I'm going to live in Maine, I need to be able to take care of things like that on my own."

Sliding his stack into place, he added hers and pinned her with a curious look. "So you're really dug in here, then? No more hanging out with the jet-setters on the Riviera?"

"No more," she confirmed with a smile. "These days, I'm more interested in sledding and having quiet dinners with my friends."

When she patted his arm, he understood she was including their simple dinner the other night in that list. Resting a hand over hers, he gave a gentle squeeze. "It's good that you're happy."

"What about you, Nick?" she asked quietly. "Could you be happy here?"

He'd fled his tiny hometown years ago, anxious to escape his father's condemning presence and the awful memory of Ian's death. But now, with Julia's help, he'd begun making peace with his past. Each day since his visit to the cemetery, he felt its grip on him loosening a little more. Before too much longer, he was confident he'd be able to think of his big brother with a smile.

While he considered her question, he was pleasantly surprised to discover the idea of staying didn't make him want to bolt. Looking into those incredible eyes, he sensed his heart leaning toward her, reaching for something he'd once thought he'd never find.

"I don't know." Looking down, he twined his fingers through hers because he liked the way it felt. "Maybe."

Tipping his chin up with her finger, she met his gaze with an understanding one of her own. She added one of her beautiful smiles and covered their joined hands with her other one. "I'll take a maybe."

As she headed back inside, Nick couldn't get over her casual acceptance of his hedging. In his experience, most women wanted a firm answer, yes or no. Then again, Julia was as different from the other women he'd known as someone could get. That she wasn't pushing him for some kind of commitment he wasn't quite ready to give was a refreshing change.

When all the gifts were loaded, Nick got Julia settled in the passenger seat and belted himself in beside her. As he started the engine, he joked, "I still can't believe I'm doing this. I feel like I should be driving a bunch of reindeer instead of an SUV."

"In an SUV or a sleigh, you've come a long way from the first day I met you," she agreed while she found some Christmas carols on the radio. "It's quite a turnaround."

After pulling onto Main Street, he smiled over at her. "You had a lot to do with it."

"Sometimes people need a little persuasion to see things differently."

"Did you use some of your father's tricks on me?" When she didn't respond, he knew he'd hit that one dead-on. Now he understood he hadn't stood much of a chance against the experienced ambassador's well-meaning protégée. A lightbulb went off in his mind, and he groaned. "That's why you suggested doing this bio series. You wanted me to stay in town and make up with my dad."

He'd expected a denial or some convoluted set of excuses that would make him angry all over again. Instead, she connected with him in the rear-view mirror, her eyes a calm, clear blue. "Yes."

Her direct answer cooled his spiking temper, but it didn't explain much. "Why? I mean, why go out of your way like that? You hardly even knew me."

"At first, I meant it to be a gift for your family. For Lainie, your parents, the kids. In spite of what your father claimed, they all wanted you back in their lives, and I asked God to help me make it happen. When you and I started getting to know each other, I knew it was the right thing, for all of you."

Nick had no clue what to think of her stunning revelation. They reached their first stop, and he got out to open the tailgate for her. Fortunately, the gifts were small so she could manage them on her own. He closed the back and waited for her in the warm cab. While he sat there trying to absorb what she'd told him, her words echoed in his mind.

I asked God to help me make it happen.

Leaning his head back, he stared out at the darkening sky. "I thought You were done with me. Was I wrong?"

A hazy shaft of light broke through the clouds, and he followed it down to where it brightened the grimy snow ahead. Just beyond that pile was the entrance to the cemetery, and even though his mind rejected the idea, in his heart he knew that was his answer.

Going to honor Ian had put him back on the path his father had spoken about the other morning. Furious and grieving, Nick had turned his back on his faith and done everything in his power to get on with his life. Now, he realized that while he'd given up on God, the feeling wasn't mutual.

God was still there, waiting for him. All he had to do was keep going in this direction, and he'd end up where he needed to be.

The passenger door opened, jolting him from his thoughts. When Julia sat down, he said, "All set?"

"Yes. One house down, forty to go."

"There's way more than forty presents back there."

"More than one child lives at a lot of the houses," she explained patiently. "That's why there are so many."

"Then we'd better get a move on. If we're late for Christmas Eve service, I'll never hear the end of it."

"Kids on Christmas Eve," Lainie muttered while she stitched up the torn hem on Mary's dress. "They're wound tighter than a hundred little springs."

Julia laughed. "There's only twenty of them."

"Could've fooled me." Glancing up, her friend added, "You really love all this, don't you?"

"Ever since I can remember, I've gone to Christmas services in the world's most incredible cathedrals," Julia replied, "but I've never been part of the entertainment. Working with the kids has been fun, and I'm looking forward to seeing how it all turns out."

"Are you heading out to Cooper and Bree's party afterward?"

"Straight from here. Nick volunteered us to help set up."

"Really?" Clearly astounded, Lainie stopped midstitch and frowned. "That doesn't sound like him at all."

"Maybe he's starting his New Year's resolution early."

She laughed. "More like he's trying to impress you. I don't know what your secret is, but he's like a different guy."

From up front, Julia heard a few tentative chords on the organ and looked over to find Nick seated there. She'd gotten accustomed to seeing him at the piano, but the sight of him in front of the multilevel organ was a huge surprise. Beside him sat Hannah, dressed for her starring role as the lead angel, her halo waving as she bounced excitedly in place.

Leaning over, he whispered something to her,

and she dutifully reached up to turn to the next page of music. He was so wonderful with her, Julia thought. She could only imagine what a wonderful father he'd be someday.

The thought had popped up out of nowhere, and she quickly pushed it away. Although Nick's recent change of heart had given her reason to hope that he was finally seeing the light, it would be foolish of her to spin daydreams around a future that might never come to be.

Since Julia's group of shepherds and animals seemed to be under control, she strolled toward the organ to find out what was going on.

"Before you ask," Nick said before she could open her mouth, "no, I don't really know how to play this beast. But the usual organist is down with the flu, so Mom shanghaied me. Again."

He was scowling, but the glimmer in his eyes gave him away, and Julia laughed. "I'm no expert, but it sounds to me like you play it just fine."

Obviously thrilled with her new position, Hannah piped up, "I'm helping Uncle Nick run over the music."

"Run through it, munchkin," he corrected her with a laugh. Glancing up at Julia, he added, "I'm a total klutz with the pedals, so don't listen too closely."

The pageant director appeared in the back of the chapel, clapping her hands to get people's attention. "It's almost showtime, kids! Everyone back here with me, please!"

Like a flash, Hannah was gone, and Nick groaned. "Great. I need another hand for the pages."

"How about this one?" Julia asked, waving hers to make the sterling-silver jingle bells ring.

Grinning as if she'd just told him he'd won a Ferrari, he slid over to make room for her on the bench. "That'd be a big help. Thanks."

All those violin lessons came in handy, allowing Julia to follow the four lines of music while he played. Paying close attention, she turned the pages as smoothly as she could to avoid distracting him. She might be biased, but she thought he was doing an excellent job, especially considering the short notice he'd gotten from his mother.

When the choir began warming up, she noticed Ann at the piano, giving them the appropriate chords. "Are you going to play both tonight?"

"Mom's handling the piano," he replied with a wry grin. "Apparently, it's not impossible for her to take care of that after all. It was her sneaky way of getting me to do something I didn't want to do."

He angled a chiding look at Julia, and she

barely managed to smother a grin. "I'm sure I have no idea what you're referring to."

"Uh-huh. Fortunately for you, I don't mind. Much."

He added a quick wink, and she couldn't help laughing even as she scolded him. "We're in church. Mind your manners."

"Yes, ma'am."

From the corner of her eye, she noticed Ben and Craig stomping off their boots in the entryway. Nick glanced up, trading a not-so-subtle nod with his friend. It got her curiosity humming. What were they up to?

Before she could ask, she saw Pastor McHenry coming up the side steps that led to the hand-carved podium. When their eyes met, his showed surprise, then his face broke into a warm, approving smile. He strolled across the stage, pausing in front of the organ. "This is a pleasant sight."

"I need three hands for this," Nick explained. "Julia volunteered."

"I heard you two made quite the impression around town today, delivering all those presents."

Nick grinned. "Yeah, some of those folks looked like they'd seen Bigfoot or something when I showed up at their door with presents."

"I'm proud of you, son," Daniel said quietly. "And you should be proud of yourself."

Nick's smile faded, but the expression that took its place wasn't angry or sad. It was content, which was something Julia had seldom seen in him. "Thanks, Dad. That means a lot to me."

"Will you both be joining us at Lainie's tomorrow?"

"Eight o'clock sharp," Nick replied with a chuckle. "Orders from the princess herself."

"Wonderful. I'm looking forward to having everyone together on Christmas morning."

The pastor included them both in a fatherly smile before heading over to speak with the choir. Once he was gone, Nick murmured, "Amazing. A few days ago, I thought I'd never hear him say that."

Julia wanted to hug him then and there, but she held back out of respect for their surroundings. "Now that you have, how does it feel?"

"Weird. But good," he added quickly. "Really good."

Before long, the church was so full there was nowhere left to sit. Standing, Ann sent Nick a questioning look, and he nodded back. She motioned for the stage manager to dim the lights, then sat down and cued her singers to start "The Little Drummer Boy."

Down the side aisles of the small church, several older children marched solemnly, holding up battery-operated candles that glowed in the subdued lighting. As they passed by the tall side windows, the beams were reflected by the stained glass, adding warm colors to the traditional procession.

From her seat, Julia subtly held up a hand to signal the lead shepherd on her side to stop, and the others lined up behind him. When they were all evenly spaced, the wise men started down the center aisle, carrying their gifts for the newborn Jesus. They paused just short of the manger, staring up at the star Ben had suspended from one of the ceiling beams. Right on time, the preset dimmer he'd installed increased the beam coming from it, sending that light to every corner of the chapel.

The effect was stunning, and a murmur of approval went through the congregation. That was the sign for Hannah to make her entrance, and she all but floated down the center of the church, stopping in the middle of all those people to give the speech she'd practiced so many times.

"Rejoice! This night our savior, Jesus Christ, is born. Let us adorn him." There was a quiet ripple of laughter, and she rolled her eyes at the mistake. "Let us *adore* him."

Beside her, Nick was shaking with barely restrained laughter, and Julia elbowed him in the ribs. Unfortunately, her effort backfired, and he choked with the effort of keeping quiet to avoid embarrassing his niece. Leaning in, he whispered, "She never once messed up that line until now."

"It was adorable," Julia whispered back. "Now hush."

When Hannah glanced over at them, Julia smiled encouragement, getting a bright grin in return. Once Hannah was in her place on the steps above the stable, Mary and Joseph made their entrance, accompanied by a flock of angels. In the manger, Mary pulled back a wool blanket and clasped her hands together melodramatically, sending a joyful look up into Heaven. "Thank You, Lord, for giving Your son to save us all."

Everyone, from wise man to shepherd, went down on their knees, hands extended in welcome to the baby in the manger.

Julia's vision blurred, and she blinked back tears. During a lifetime of traveling, she'd witnessed Christmas reenactments much grander than this. But here, in this humble chapel in northern Maine, was the first one to affect her so deeply. The simple costumes and setting made it feel real, closer to the truth than any of the other, more lavish scenes.

But more than that—it was the appreciation of the people watching their children and grandchildren act out a story that took place so long ago. The day that God pledged His only son as the savior of His people.

That was love, Julia thought, offering up a silent prayer of gratitude. A father's love.

When Nick's hand closed over hers, she glanced over to see his head bowed, eyes closed in a reverence that both amazed and touched her. It seemed the black sheep had finally found his way home.

On this very special night filled with blessings, nothing could have been more perfect.

Nick didn't realize he'd reached for Julia's hand until he felt her clasping his back. What had possessed him to do that—in church, no less—was beyond him, but now that he'd gone there, it felt right. More than right, actually.

Perfect.

As the ceiling lights gradually came back up, he played the opening chords of "Hark the Herald Angels Sing," which brought everyone to their feet. Slightly off-key in places, the congregation worked their way through every verse with gusto. From his spot, Nick saw his parents at the front of the choir, holding hands while they sang from memory.

Seeing them that way, he flashed back to the Christmas Eve services he'd attended as a child. Only this time, the memories he'd buried for so many years made him smile. Sitting here in his father's church, Nick finally felt at peace. More than that, he felt at home, and he was grateful to God for welcoming him back after all this time.

When the music died away, Dad strolled to mid-stage and held his arms out as if he were embracing the entire parish at once. "Merry Christmas." Everyone echoed the sentiment, and he continued. "On this night, we celebrate not only the birth of Jesus, but of every child who comes into our world. Whatever their circumstances, whatever their nationality or creed, every new soul brings with it the hope of a better future for us all."

This was nothing like the sermons he remembered, and Nick found himself fascinated by the bold direction the pastor had chosen. What should have been a solemn, traditional lesson became a celebration of the children who'd participated in the pageant, working together to tell the story of Jesus's birth.

"Inspiring," Dad said, winging a smile around the packed church to every kid dressed in a costume. "You captured the wonder of this night perfectly, and I applaud you all."

When he began clapping, people looked at each other with the same confusion Nick was feeling right now. Clapping in church? Daniel McHenry's church? Unheard of, but he was hearing it all the same and was the first to join in. A few at a time, others did the same until the chapel echoed with applause. Odd, but heartwarming, he mused with a grin. Who'd have guessed his very conservative father had it in him?

From there, Dad focused on the Christmas story that had been told and retold for over two thousand years. But he had one more trick up the sleeve of his choir robe, and he saved it for last.

"No matter where we are, how far we might have wandered from our Heavenly Father," he said in a comforting voice, "He sees us. In a manger in Bethlehem, or in a high-rise office or on a fishing trawler, God is always with us. When we look to Him in faith, with humility in our hearts, He will open His kingdom to us and keep us in His grace forever."

Nick wasn't singled out in any way, but he instantly recognized that the closing of that sermon was meant for him. In that crowded church, his father had devised a way to reach him personally. Not long ago, he'd have rejected a message like that as a manipulative attempt to bring him back into the fold.

Now he treasured it because it was more than words a small-town preacher had strung together to make a point. His father honestly believed what he was saying, and Nick found himself believing it, too.

"'A few friends,' Cooper said," Bree complained to Julia while they mixed more fruit juice and ginger ale for the punch. "I should've remembered the first time he said that, and two hundred people showed up here for the Fourth of July."

Julia laughed. "I think it's great that the first party you're hosting as a married couple is on Christmas Eve. What better way to start?"

"Oh, you're right," Bree agreed quickly, the diamonds on her left hand sparkling as she swiped a piece of curly hair out of her eyes. "Cooper loves all this, but I'm not much of a party person. I'll get used to it. Eventually."

The final word came on a sarcastic note, obviously intended for her husband as he joined them in the kitchen. Putting an arm around her, he kissed her temple. "Quit complaining. You know you love it."

"I love you," she replied with an adoring smile. "That's why I'm such a good sport."

"Oh, yeah?" He laughed. "We got the tree you wanted, the huge wreath and six different kinds of wrapping paper. Sammy's even wearing a big red bow on his collar. I'd say we're the good sports."

Julia enjoyed hearing them banter this way. Bright and obviously in love, the Landrys proved that opposite personalities could coexist very happily. She couldn't help wondering if she and Nick might be able to make it work, too. His demeanor during church was encouraging, and she no longer considered a lasting relationship between them a lost cause.

Now she saw a glimmer of hope. If only he'd stay a little longer, they might actually have a chance.

"Are you mixing or pouring?"

A gruff voice dragged Julia away from her wandering thoughts to the present. When she noticed Mavis Freeman standing in front of the table, she greeted the elderly lighthouse keeper with a smile. "Pouring," she replied, ladling some into a glass cup for her. "Merry Christmas, Mrs. Freeman."

"I've told you at least a hundred times, it's Mavis. Unless you cross me, and then it don't matter what you call me 'cause I won't be listening."

The bluster made Julia laugh, since everyone in town knew the woman had a soft heart. "I'll keep that in mind. Thank you again for your donation to the Gifting Tree. Nick and I delivered the toys earlier today, and there will be a very happy little artist tomorrow morning, thanks to you."

"Wasn't much, but you're welcome." After a sip of punch, she gave Julia a puzzled look. "Did you say Nick helped you? As in Nick McHenry?"

"Yes, and yes. Some of the boxes were pretty heavy, and I appreciated the help."

The woman clucked in sympathy. "Poor boy.

He was never the same after his brother died. It was like he crawled inside himself and never came out." She gave Julia a long, knowing look. "Seems you found the way in, though. Good for you."

When Julia had first arrived in Holiday Harbor, the local gossips had flown into a tizzy, following her every move to discover why she was there and what she was up to. As a precaution, Julia kept her personal life quiet, hoping to blend in as much as possible.

Since Mavis had hit the nail so squarely, she decided to accept her interest for what it was: approval. "Thank you."

While Julia refilled her cup, Mavis said, "Trust me, honey. The toughest ones are the best in the long run. Now, I better go mingle or Bree will put me to work in the kitchen."

As she moved away from the desserts, a commotion at the door caught Julia's attention. Ben had just arrived, and he motioned to Nick from the doorway. The two old friends put their heads together, deep in conversation about something that Ben needed to explain by spreading his hands out nearly arm's length apart, then pulling them back together. Apparently, whatever they were discussing had ended well because they exchanged broad grins and a high five before joining the festivities.

It brought to mind their quick nod just before the service began. What was going on? she wondered while she added more of Mavis's famous gingerbread to the nearly empty tray. Hard as she tried, she couldn't imagine what those two had cooked up tonight of all nights.

One thing she'd learned in the past month was that Nick McHenry did nothing in a small way. Whatever it was, it was big.

Nick had never been so nervous in his life.

He'd started *Kaleidoscope* with little more than a small business loan and an idea, growing it into a national magazine with over a million readers. He'd given speeches at conferences and trade shows in front of hundreds of his colleagues, many of whom were just waiting for him to fail so they could go after the top-notch staff he'd assembled.

But the danger behind this gift was something else again because this time he'd followed his instincts out onto a different kind of limb. He was risking a very personal rejection in hopes of doing something special for the amazing woman who'd ignored every warning and wormed her way into his heart. He still wasn't sure how she'd managed it, but he couldn't deny it any longer.

Crazy as it seemed, he was in love with Julia Stanton. It had started that first day, he now realized, when he caught himself wondering how to get another one of her brilliant smiles. Despite the wrong turns he'd taken along the way, somehow he kept ending up in the same place: with her. If that wasn't a Christmas blessing, he didn't understand the concept.

As they got out in front of Toyland, he paused a moment to drink in the peaceful stillness of Christmas Eve in Holiday Harbor. Everyone had left their lights on in honor of the coming holiday, the reflections in the snow giving the town a festive glow. Nowhere was the effect more special than in the tall display windows Julia had so lovingly decorated.

Looking down at the replica village that had angered him so much only a month ago, he felt a calm he'd never expected to experience standing in the hometown he'd tried so hard to escape. Now that Julia was here, it was the only place he wanted to be.

"Would you like to come in?" she asked as she unlocked the door. "After all your help today, I'd offer you something to eat, but Bree and Cooper took care of that."

Actually, he'd been so preoccupied with his surprise, he hadn't been able to choke down more than a couple of crab puffs. Too late, it had occurred to him that he'd never actually seen the present he'd worked so hard to arrange. The builder had assured him it was the right scale for her furniture, but that was only the start of Nick's concerns. What if she hated it? What if it was the wrong style? He wasn't a toy connoisseur like her, and he knew next to nothing about miniature interior decorating.

When he noticed her eyeing him strangely, he realized he hadn't answered her question. Feeling like a moron, he plastered on a smile. "Sure. Sounds good."

"What sounds good?"

"Coming in." Her expression told him he'd missed the mark with his response, but he did his best to shrug it off. "It's either that or Lainie'll rope me into helping her and Todd put together the kids' toys."

Julia laughed as they walked into the shop. "It's a lot of work, that's for sure. I'm a lot faster at it now than I used to be."

When she opened the door to head upstairs, Shakespeare called out, "No scary monsters allowed here!"

"It's just me, you loon," she scolded lightly. To Nick, she added, "I think Hannah taught him a few new phrases while he was at their house."

"More Sesame Street than Globe Theater," he commented with a grin. "I kinda like it."

When she rounded the top of the stairs and abruptly stopped, Nick's pulse kicked into rabbit range, and he took a breath to steady his voice before speaking. "Something wrong?"

Moving forward as if she was in a trance, she whispered, "Oh, Nick. It's beautiful."

Once he could see the model for himself, he couldn't agree more. With a stately three-story main house and a two-story wing on each side, it spread across the entire long table Ben had dragged in from her study. Lights shone in every room, giving the house a welcoming glow. Crystal chandeliers in the more formal spaces gave it a classy appearance even Nick could appreciate.

From where he stood, he couldn't find the joints Ben had made while putting the house together. To him, it looked like the thing had been built right where it stood, waiting patiently for Julia to fill it with her tiny treasures.

Eyes shining with delight, she launched herself at him in an exuberant hug that nearly knocked him off his feet.

"So you like it, then?" he asked.

"It's exactly what I've always wanted."

She added a joyful laugh, and he wrapped his arms around her with a grin. "You really know how to thank a guy."

Laughing, she embraced him again, cuddling in for a hug that made him want to stand in that spot for the rest of his life. As she pulled away, he kept her circled in his arms because he liked the way it felt.

"I have something for you, too," she told him. "I was going to keep it until tomorrow, but it seems right to give it to you now."

Strolling over to the tree they'd decorated together, she picked up a package done up in shiny gold paper with a striped ribbon and bow. Grinning, he shook the present the way they'd joked about earlier. "It's a Ferrari."

Tilting her head, she gave him the chiding look he'd come to enjoy so much. For some reason, he got a charge out of getting that reaction from the classiest woman he'd ever known. "Some people might think it's better than a fancy sports car."

"Nothing's better than a Ferrari," he retorted as he ripped it open. When he saw what was inside, he had to look again to be sure he wasn't mistaken the first time. "It's your first edition of *A Christmas Carol.*"

"No, it's *your* first edition of *A Christmas Carol.* When I first met you, you called yourself Scrooge, remember?"

"It fit."

"Not anymore," she assured him with a warm smile. "Under all that cool, you have a wonderful, generous heart. I'm so glad you let me close enough to see it."

"I didn't even know it was there until I met

you." Cradling her cheek in his hand, he added, "No one ever tried as hard with me as you have. I love you."

He held his breath, dreading her response. Awkward as it felt to say those words, it would be even worse if she didn't share his feelings.

Resting her hand over his, she looked up at him with shining eyes. "And I love you. Merry Christmas, Nick."

For the first time in years, that phrase meant something to him beyond an automatic response. Leaning in for a kiss, he whispered, "Merry Christmas, Julia."

Chapter Twelve

The day after Christmas, Nick stopped at Julia's in the morning to say goodbye.

The sinking feeling she'd had in her chest since Christmas Eve had deepened throughout the weekend, despite her determined efforts to wish it away. But now there was no way around it. Nick was leaving, and she had to let him go.

His dark eyes were shadowed, as if he hadn't slept any better than she had last night. When they met hers, he looked as unhappy as she felt. After a long hug, he held her at arms' length with a hopeful expression. "You could come with me."

She'd been dreading this moment. Much as she wanted to be with him, she couldn't follow in her mother's footsteps and give up her independence for a man. Not even a man she loved with all her heart. "My business is here, not to mention my friends and the roots I've always wanted to have.

I can't give all that up when I've finally found the place where I want to be."

"I know."

He was so downcast, she nearly relented just to see him smile. But she held firm and suggested, "You could stay and run *Kaleidoscope* from here. When we were delivering gifts the other day, you said 'maybe.' Have you changed your mind?"

When he looked away, she knew the answer. He might love her, but like her, he wasn't willing to upend his life to be a part of someone else's. Better to find that out now, she supposed, than in a few months when he regretted choosing her and left anyway. She'd only love him more then, and it would be that much harder to accept his decision.

Resting a hand on his cheek, she gave him the smile she wanted him to remember her wearing. "Thank you for everything, Nick. Have a good trip back."

With that, she forced herself to lightly kiss his cheek and turn away. She didn't dare look back, but she hoped he might have a last-minute change of heart. She walked into her office and sat at her desk, staring at the mini cuckoo clock her parents had sent her for Christmas while she waited for him to come in after her.

He never did.

* * *

Nick wasn't one for big New Year's resolutions and celebrations, but this year had started out with a thud. Glaring out the window into the dark, he was convinced he was the only one home in the entire condo complex tonight. Laboring over the final installment of Julia's biography hadn't helped his mood any. All week he'd tried to finish the draft so he could have it polished in plenty of time, but he kept running into writer's block.

Too short, too long, too mushy, too cold. He just couldn't seem to get the tone right, and it was driving him insane. The problem was, every time he tried to fix it, his mind drifted off on tangents that had nothing to do with the article. Her graceful way of moving, the lilt of her voice, how he'd do anything to make her smile. That's when he caught himself staring at the picture of the two of them he'd framed for his desk. Lainie had taken it when they were sledding, and they were both grinning like little kids, their cheeks pink with the cold. The most fun he'd had in years, that day was so vivid for him, he could almost feel the sting of snow on his face.

Since then, he'd been stinging for an entirely different reason. He'd finally fallen in love, but when push came to shove, he'd chosen the safe route he'd been on for years. Their emotional Christmas Eve was still fresh in his mind, and he couldn't get the images—or the feelings—out of his head. It had been the best night of his life, and he'd walked away from it like it never happened. Yes, he'd made a token effort to have her come with him, but he'd asked her knowing that she'd say no.

For that mistake alone, he deserved to be miserable.

When his cell phone rang, he picked it up so he'd have something else to focus on.

Julia.

Startled and thrilled all at once, he nearly fumbled the thing onto the floor. When he finally got a firm grip on it, he took a breath to steady his voice before answering. "Hey, there."

Her voice was like music over the sketchy connection. "Hey, yourself. I assumed you'd be out, but I wanted to wish you a Happy New Year."

Was it? Not really, but he didn't want to burden her with that. "Thanks. To you, too."

"Nick, what's wrong?"

Several responses passed through his mind, none of them the least bit helpful. *I love you. I miss you. Please forgive me and take me back because I can't stand being without you anymore.*

Because none of those were an option, he went with, "Nothing, just trying to get this edition polished up."

"I'll let you go, then. Happy New Year."

After they hung up, he threw his head back and glared up at the ceiling. What was wrong with him? He'd never let anything stand in his way when he wanted something, so why now? He mulled that over for a few minutes, then came up with an answer.

This time, his heart was at stake. To be truly happy, he needed to take that final leap, and it scared him to death. Not only for himself, but for Julia. If things between them didn't work out and he hurt her more than he already had, he'd never be able to forgive himself. It wasn't good, he grumbled to himself, but it was an answer. And it was the truth. So what was he going to do about it?

Closing his eyes, he murmured a humble request for help. God was a lot smarter than him, and for something this big, Nick trusted His judgment more than his own. Suddenly, the solution to the problem he'd been wrestling with since leaving Holiday Harbor was as clear as if someone had written it down for him, and he smiled up at the ceiling. "Thanks."

Picking up his phone again, he thumbed through the list for his IT guru, a fellow night owl. "Frankie, how's it goin'?"

"I've been trying to reach you," he replied in a nervous voice. "Did you know the issue's not up yet?"

"Yeah, I'm still tweaking. Listen, I'm thinking about making some changes. Are you still interested in taking over my condo?"

The 40th Annual Holiday Harbor Snowball Dance was in full swing.

It was mid-January, and after being cooped up inside for so long, people were more than ready for a night out. From her post at the baked-goods table, Julia watched laughing couples navigating the waltz, the fox trot and some dances that were apparently local inventions with no names. In addition to the fun everyone was having, the proceeds would pay for a new roof over the lighthouse parlor. Mavis had told Julia she was using so many of her pots and pans for leaks, she had none left for cooking.

A few men around town had asked Julia to the dance, but she'd politely declined. It had been a busy month for Toyland, and she wasn't up to being entertaining. At least that's what she told Lainie when her nosy friend asked her why she didn't have a date.

The truth was, she missed Nick. He'd been gone long enough that she should have gotten over their brief romance, but her heart refused to let him go. He'd done a marvelous job on her biography, and she'd nearly called to congratulate him. But in light of his cool reaction to her New Year's call, she'd decided not to contact him again. Obviously, he'd chosen to move on without her, and she knew she should do the same.

Easier said than done, she thought with a sigh, crouching down to get another plate of fudge from the shelves under the table.

"I forgot how much I hate this hokey town nonsense."

The sound of Nick's grumbling shocked her so much, she banged her head on the underside of the table. Holding the fudge in one hand and rubbing her head with the other, she carefully stood to stare at him. "What are you doing here?"

With that maddening gleam in his eyes, he shrugged. "Heard there was a dance, so I thought I'd come check it out. I don't like 'em myself, but readers love a good, old-fashioned sock hop."

Her delighted heart was lodged firmly in her throat, but she decided to play along with his cool-kid demeanor. Rearranging the treats to make room for the fudge, she asked, "You came all the way from Virginia for this?"

"Actually, I came all the way from Virginia for you."

His nonchalant tone did nothing to mask the emotion humming in those words, and Julia glanced up to find him gazing at her with the adoring look she'd missed so much. Holding out his hand, he smiled. "Dance with me?"

From out of nowhere, Lainie popped into the scene. "You two go on. I'll take over here."

While Nick led her out to the floor, Julia eyed him suspiciously. "You set me up."

"Well, yeah. I knew you'd be helping out, 'cause you always do, so I had to cover my bases." As he settled his arms around her, he said, "It feels good to do this again."

She agreed wholeheartedly, but she wasn't letting him off the hook quite that easily. Squirming free, she took his left hand and guided his right to her waist in proper ballroom form. "Tell me what you've been up to the past few weeks."

Understanding flashed across his features, and his expression dimmed considerably. "Being miserable, mostly."

"Why is that?"

"Because you weren't there."

"Nick, we discussed this—"

"I know," he interrupted, "and I didn't mean that the way it came out. I don't expect you to drop everything you've got here for me."

"Good, because that's not happening." Hearing the uncharacteristic bite in her voice, she softencd her approach. "But I missed you, too, more than I can say. By the way, you did a wonderful job with the ending of my story. It was perfect."

"With such a great subject, how could I go wrong? I enjoyed it so much, I'm thinking of hiring an assistant so I can write more of my own pieces."

That sounded nothing like the man who'd first landed in town back in November. "Really? What happened to running the show?"

"Oh, I'll still be in charge. But I have to admit, those few days I took off at the end of the year were kinda nice, and I wouldn't mind doing that more often."

"Good for you." She approved heartily. "So what are you planning to do with all your spare time?"

"Is that a new dress?"

She recognized the sidestep but decided to let him get away with it for now. "Mom sent it from Milan. She said it was new silk for spring, but I couldn't wait. Do you like it?"

With his finger, he motioned for her to spin so he could get the full effect. When she stopped in front of him, his grin widened as he resumed his very proper dancing pose. "Fantastic. Were you able to send them that first payment check you were talking about?"

The memory of that conversation made her feel more than proud. It reinforced her belief that she had the skill and determination she needed to make her own way in the world. As their only child, Julia knew she'd have to continue pressing her parents to accept her newfound independence.

But in the end, they'd understand why it was so important to her and would go along. It might take them a while, and would be much harder on them than on her. Fortunately, she was a very patient person.

"Dad wanted to rip it up, but I told him I'd just keep sending them until he gave in and cashed them. I did my books beforehand, so I also sent them my profit and loss statement for last year. It felt so good to start paying them back and prove to them that Toyland is doing really well, even now that the holidays are over. You were right about the articles being good for business."

"You've accomplished a lot since moving here. I'm sure you've impressed a lot of people."

"Including you?" When he didn't answer, she nudged. "Be honest, now. When you first met me, you probably thought I'd be out of business in a month."

He held up two fingers in a V, and she gasped in dismay. "Two months?"

"Well, you opened just before Christmas. How hard can it be to run a toy store that time of year?"

She opened her mouth to inform him that it had been incredibly difficult, but the humor gleaming in his eyes told her he was ribbing her. "I'll get you for that one."

"Really? How?"

Retaliation wasn't really her strength, but she

glowered at him for all she was worth. "I'll think of something."

Clearly unfazed, he threw his head back in a carefree laugh that turned more than a few heads. One of them was Bree's, and she promptly snapped a picture of them with her phone.

"Landry," he threatened her with a stern finger, "if that ends up online, you are so fired."

"Whatever." Flouncing a shoulder, she sashayed away with Cooper, who sent his buddy a sympathetic look over his shoulder.

"You have such a way with people," Julia teased. "What's your secret?"

"Always keep 'em guessing." The band started the opening chords of a classic waltz, and she finally let him draw her into his arms. Looking down at her intently, he said, "I have a confession to make."

His sudden shift in mood was unsettling, to say the least. "It must be important."

"It is." After a moment, he said, "I talked to your dad yesterday."

"Oh, no." She hadn't mentioned Nick's leaving to her parents, so her mother probably still thought they were an item. "He didn't have you put under surveillance, did he?"

"No." Thinking it over, he chuckled. "At least, I don't think so."

Just in case it occurred to him, Julia made a

note to speak to her father directly about not interfering in Nick's life. "Then what did he call you about?"

"He didn't. I called him."

Reaching into his pocket, Nick took out the sort of blue velvet box every girl hoped to get someday. He flipped it open with his thumb, and the diamonds inside sparkled in the lights from the mirrored ball spinning overhead. "I'm not the down-on-one-knee kinda guy, but I love you, Julia. Will you marry me?"

"Yes," she breathed instinctively. It felt so wonderful she repeated it, feeling a little light-headed as Nick slid the beautiful setting onto her finger.

She held it out for him to see, and he took her hand in his, brushing a kiss over the back. "Gorgeous."

Unable to speak, she simply nodded, smiling as he sealed his proposal with a kiss. After being cautious for so long, it felt wonderful to throw all that aside and jump into the future.

With Nick.

* * * * *

Dear Reader,

I absolutely *love* the holidays! Hectic as they can be, I enjoy having everyone together at home and visiting both sides of our extended family. We haul out those old movies, cue up the Christmas music and make sure there are plenty of everyone's favorite goodies on hand. Even though the kids are older now, they still have fun cutting down a tree and pulling their collection of ornaments out of the bins. To my amazement, they still remember where each one came from. Those moments are precious, and I know they won't last forever. I always make it a point to take time off at the end of the year to just relax and soak everything in.

Besides the traditional family surroundings of Holiday Harbor, this story includes some elements from one of my favorite classics *A Christmas Carol*. Whether it's the original or a modern adaptation, I adore the concept that no matter how curmudgeon-y you are, with a little help you can change your perspective and embrace the joy that's going on all around you. Fortunately for Nick, Julia isn't nearly as scary as Scrooge's ghosts.

If you'd like to stop by for a visit, you'll find me online at *www.miaross.com,* Facebook and

Twitter. It would be great to hear from you, so while you're there, send me a message in your favorite format.

Merry Christmas!
Mia Ross

Questions For Discussion

1. At the beginning of the story, Nick and Julia are familiar with each other but have never met. If you've been in a similar situation, what perceptions had you and the other person formed before meeting? Were they accurate?

2. Julia loves Christmas, and she's excited to be part of the festivities in Holiday Harbor. Thinking back to your first Christmas in a new home, what are your favorite memories?

3. Nick has avoided coming home for many years but finally gives in and returns for Thanksgiving. Have you known anyone in this kind of situation? How did they handle it?

4. Because he lives alone and works so much, Nick is far removed from the holiday whirl. His niece's excitement about decorating gets to him, and he reluctantly agrees to participate, then ends up enjoying himself. Do you know someone who shuns this part of Christmas? Why do you think that is?

5. Even though Nick isn't fond of children in general, he can appreciate the fanciful holiday setting Julia chose for Toyland. Are you

inspired by seasonal decorations and music? Which do you like the best?

6. Julia's last relationship ended in disaster, both personally and financially. Do you know anyone who was betrayed by someone they trusted? How did they handle it?

7. For years Nick has blamed himself for his brother's death, and it's altered his own life. Have you ever done something that haunted you for a long time? What did you do to get past it?

8. At the beginning of the story, Nick believes that God no longer cares about him. Do you know anyone like that? What do you think it would take to convince them otherwise?

9. Julia admires her mother's ability to be her bright, bubbly self, no matter what anyone else might think of her. Most of us aren't quite that confident, but what could you do to be more like that?

10. Despite the fabulous life she's led, Julia has always longed for a place to call home. Do you know someone who seems to have everything but wants something just out of reach?

11. During the Christmas pageant, world-traveler Julia is touched by the honest, down-to-earth nature of the Safe Harbor Church and its congregation. What are some of the impressions you get in your own church during this season?

12. Nick and Julia's Christmas gifts to each other come straight from the heart. Can you think of gifts you've received that made the same kind of impact?